...AND SOME
OF THEM ARE DEAD

A Short Story Anthology

Compiled & Edited by

Victoria Heckman & Margaret Searles

Deadly Alibi Press Ltd.
Vancouver, Washington USA

Library of Congress Control Number: 2002106426

Deadly Alibi Press Ltd.
PO Box 5947
Vancouver, WA 98661-5947
http://www.deadlyalibipress.com/
email: editor30@attbi.com

Deadly Alibi Press thanks each of the authors below for their contribution to this anthology.

AND SOME OF THEM ARE DEAD

INTRODUCTION

AND SOME OF THEM ARE DEAD, the third anthology compiled by members of the Central Coast Chapter of Sisters in Crime, is a collection of mysteries, not all of them murders, in a variety of settings. We've got everything from cozy to hard-boiled to historical. The authors who have contributed are superb at the short story and excel at capturing the reader in just a few pages. You may be surprised to note that some of our "Sisters" are men! We have more surprises in store, so get comfortable, turn the page, and let yourself be captured . . .

Victoria Heckman
President, Central Coast Chapter
Sisters in Crime

AND SOME OF THEM ARE DEAD

TABLE OF CONTENTS

BACK IN THE SADDLE

by Victoria Heckman

"If you report me, then I'll make sure the board finds out about your joint ownership. They'll wonder why you neglected to tell them that little detail."

"So it was you! What did you come here for? To rub it in? I don't know you from Adam. You should have kept it that way. You could lose your job, or face criminal charges. What about your wife?"

"She already knows. She wants me to give it to you. I won't. Then what will I have? I think you have more to lose than I do if this comes out. Not only the funding, but what if you have to pay back what you've already taken? And how are you going to look to your little community when they find out you both lied to them?"

A response I couldn't understand.

"Don't you threaten me! I'll expose you, I swear I will." The argument continued, in fierce whispers. I couldn't tell who the speakers were, but at least one was male—the one with the wife, I expertly deduced. I was interested but exhausted, and only half-awake. Was this a realistic dream?

* * *

I'm not going to make it, I thought. Oh, my God, I'm not going to make it! And I didn't. I smacked face first into the butt of the rented horse and slithered to the ground. I got up quickly to see if any of the other trail riders had witnessed my shame. Nope. Good. I dusted off my blue jeans and assessed my butt as best I could.

I have always loved horses and riding, although it had been more years than I cared to count since I had ridden.

Why I chose to mount with a running leap over the back end of this patient, unsuspecting animal eludes me. Too many John Wayne movies as a kid, I guess. At least this horse didn't startle easily. That had to be a plus.

It was a beautiful morning. The weather report had threatened rain on this first day of our "cowboy retreat weekend," as the tourist brochure put it.

Our trail-boss, Chips McAllister, flapped toward me in his "Pale Rider" long coat and chaps. Chaps! "Howdy."

"Uh, howdy?" You've got to be kidding.

"It's Ms. Marshall, isn't it?"

"Yes, but call me Max." It's Maxine, but I like Max better. Chips had a very nice smile, what I could see of it under the Sam Elliot soup-strainer. He looked about my age, 40ish, and in great shape. I might get to like chaps. Beneath a sweat-stained Stetson strings of dark hair hung past his collar. Altogether, not a bad picture of the All-American cowboy; the look he was going for no doubt, since he did represent Greenhorn Trailrides outside Craig, Colorado.

"Get ready to mount up, ma'am, we're leaving in five minutes." He eyed my dusty figure, a twinkle in his eyes. "Need a leg up?"

"No, thanks. I can manage." I felt my face pink up. No more stupid stunts. I would be an able-bodied hand for the entire three day trip if it killed me.

I mounted the chestnut mare, Blossom, handily turned her, and watched Chips help Natalie Hosley mount. Natalie stuck her foot in the left stirrup, her arms stretched for the saddle horn. Chips laced his fingers to support her right foot. He was well-braced, but Natalie was very short and round.

Bob Hosley pushed Natalie's rear. "You can do it, just a little farther."

Chips said, "Mr. Hosley, I can he'p the little lady up if you'll step back, sir."

Bob pushed harder and elbowed Chips, who stepped back to keep his balance. Natalie shrieked and did midair splits, compressing Bob under her full weight. Miraculously, everyone held on. In another moment, Natalie beamed down from her hard-earned perch atop Checkers, the smallest mare.

Bob grunted onto a roan named Bubbles. The three other riders managed to mount with less excitement.

Chips rode a beautiful black gelding he called Arthur. He guided Arthur toward a flat, open, grassless plain. With varying degrees of skill, we followed, single file, although there was room to re-enact a cavalry charge. For the first half mile or so, the horses dragged their feet, turned their heads longingly back toward the stable, and hung their noses to the ground to search for the single blade of grass left in the county. The Hosleys followed and I rode behind Bob's Bubbles. As a last ditch sign of rebellion, Bubbles emitted an enormous noxious-smelling cloud from her posterior. She was well-named.

An older gentleman (older than me), on the grey gelding just behind me, coughed. "Man! What the hell is that? It's okay, Phaeton, take it easy, boy."

I think he said Phaeton. It could have been "Fat One," not a nice name for a horse. I turned and smiled at him. When he looked at me like I might be responsible for the odor, I pointed and said, "Bubbles."

He nodded and smiled. "John Raintree. From New Mexico."

"Max Marshall. California."

We rode on and I sank into the lethargy of riding a walking horse. Chips did nothing to break up the monotony. No snappy patter, no tourist tips, no anecdotes. The two young college types bringing up the rear laughed a great deal, but stayed a distance apart.

After a couple of eternity-hours, the terrain became more interesting—grass! Eventually we came to some brushy hills. The ride had begun after lunch, but I was hungry and ready to stop.

Chips read my mind. "Okay, everyone. Pull up a sec." He waited while we clumped around him. The horses lowered their heads and began to crop the low grass. Checkers, with Natalie aboard, wandered to a low branch and lipped leaves.

Chips said, "Don't let them eat with their bridles on." Right.

Checkers wandered into the undergrowth and Natalie said, "Checkers, you're a bad girl. Stop that, now." She tugged ineffectually on the reins. Only Checkers' hindquarters were visible, and Natalie seemed to float atop the shrubbery.

Chips dragged the reluctant Checkers from the bushes and told Natalie, "Show her who's boss. She won't act up if she knows who's in charge." Natalie nodded. We all knew who was in charge.

Chips said, "We're only a few miles from our camp. The pack horses with our provisions and equipment are meeting us there. You have water and snacks in your packs, if you need them." We dug in our saddlebags for the bottles of spring water, fresh fruit and granola bars. I was thrilled, even though I usually eat my granola bars with Diet Pepsi. I had envisioned survival on buffalo jerky and bacteria-ridden stream water.

During our brief stop, no one dismounted—probably a good thing. We continued through progressively more beautiful country until we reached our camp.

Bedrolls, blobs of nylon I assumed were tents, and cooking paraphernalia surrounded a rock fire ring, where a slim figure crouched, coaxing flames from reluctant wood. Through the smoke, I thought it was a woman, but no—a teenage boy turned to greet us. He was dressed almost identically to Chips, minus the hat, and had flaming red hair.

Chips spoke sharply. "What are you doing here?"

"I thought I'd come along and help out." The young man met his gaze.

"I told you no. What does no mean where you're from?" Chips dismounted and tied Arthur to a makeshift rail of bent branches.

I knew I was in trouble the minute my feet hit the ground. My legs folded up and I sat, right there under the stirrup. Chips started toward me, but Natalie, and then Bob, did the same thing, so he stopped to help them. John Raintree slid out of his saddle and eased me to my feet, smiling and murmuring lies about how I'd feel better in a few minutes. The two younger riders had no trouble. Curse them. They laughed and joked as they tied up at the rail.

Chips barked at the boy. "Don't just stand there! As long as you're here, make yourself useful. Unsaddle." The boy turned to Chips' horse. "Not mine. Theirs." Chips jerked his thumb toward Checkers and Bubbles.

The college types unsaddled their own. John Raintree gave me a questioning look and I nodded that I was okay. I knew how to unsaddle, but wasn't sure I could. I did loosen the girth strap around Blossom's middle, and she sighed in gratitude. I rubbed her neck and breathed in her horsy smell.

Since the age of twelve I have been smitten with horses, and on the rare occasions I was allowed to ride, I refused to bathe until the smell faded. My mother loved that. On this ride I was content to wear the same clothes for two days.

Jason! Doooon't!"

The college boy grabbed the girl and pulled her into a tight embrace. He said, "Yo, Tiff, give me a little," and tried to kiss her.

"Jason, you're all sweaty!" Tiff pushed at him. He kissed her. God.

Hobbling, I led Blossom back to the rail and Chips unsaddled her. Natalie and Bob sat on logs by the smoky fire. Bob rubbed Natalie's legs vigorously.

Chips called to the boy, "Hey, Red, take these folks and show 'em the firewood." He indicated the laughing students. Red dutifully marched them out of sight, and the camp became blissfully quiet, except for Natalie, who whimpered, "I'm so sore. I'll never walk again."

John Raintree erected tents like he knew what he was doing. I wandered over to help.

We heard the firewood gatherers long before they reached camp. How could they have so much energy at the end of the day? Red added wood to the fire, and soon wonderful smells rose from the cooking pots. The sun was low, the woods dusky blue and shadowed. Red passed out bowls of black bean chili, hunks of sourdough bread, fresh fruit, and heaven above, hot coffee and lucious, decadent chocolate chip cookies.

"Made these yourself, did you Chips?" He blushed and nodded. I bit into the best cookie I'd ever tasted. "You could give Mrs. Fields a run for her money," I said.

"Nah." Chips really was cute.

Red startled me. He poked at the fire, sending up a shower of sparks, then stomped away into the darkness.

"Hey, where are you going?" Chips called. "You know the rules. No one leaves the camp alone after dark."

Red turned and glared at Chips. "I'm going to take care of business, if that's okay with you."

Chips pursed his lips and sighed. "Okay, but don't go far."

"You don't have to watch me every second!"

Chips stared at the spot where Red had disappeared, an odd expression on his face.

"Don't you play the guitar, or something?" Tiff giggled and Jason put a proprietary arm around her. John Raintree had moved his saddle near the fire for a pillow and stretched out his long, lean form in repose. Did they hire these guys for us tourists? All we needed was a coyote howling in the distance.

Chips laid on the accent. "Wall now, purty lady, I don't rightly know how, but I got another idee. How 'bout we go around and introduce ourselves? I'm Chips McAllister, and I'm the head wrangler of Greenhorn Trailrides. I've lived in one part or another of Colorado most of my life, and I wouldn't have it any other way." He nodded to Bob Hosley.

Bob gazed down at Natalie, who dozed in the crook of his arm. "I'm Bob Hosley, and this is my wife Natalie. We're from Bettendorf, Iowa, and we've been married almost a year. We came here on vacation and decided to take this camp-out before we head back home. I'm in computers and Natalie's a housewife. We're kinda hoping to start a family soon." A flicker of distaste seemed to pass over his features. It was gone so quickly, I couldn't be sure.

The focus turned to the young people. "I'm Tiffany Ryerson, but my friends call me Tiff. I go to Colorado State University. I'm undeclared." I assumed she meant her major, and not her marital status or I.Q.

"I'm from Boulder, and I just really want to travel. I told my parents I wanted to take a year off and they just about had a cow!" More giggles. "They said they'd pay for a trip this summer if I'd go to school next year. I said okay, but only if Jason could come too!"

Red's spot was still vacant, so I was next. "I'm Max Marshall from Los Angeles. I've lived in L.A. about nine years, and before that I lived up the coast in a little town half way between L.A. and San Francisco. I'm in public relations," I lied. It wasn't a total lie. Policework involves a ton of P.R.

I looked expectantly at John. He stayed prone, eyes shut.

After a moment of silence, he spoke. "John Raintree. Shiprock, New Mexico. I just thought this would be a fun thing to do." And that was all we got out of him.

"Let's sing!" Tiff said. So we were forced to sing. Red came back in the middle of "Red River Valley," appropriately enough. He didn't rejoin our circle, but crawled into one of the tents.

Bob rose and said, "I'm going to get Natalie in the sack." The youngsters erupted into hoots of raucous laughter. He colored furiously, glared at them, and said, "I mean, you know, put her to bed. We're tired." Bob hefted her up and stuffed her into a tent. She mumbled and moaned, so I guessed she wasn't dead.

"Where's the bathroom?" Tiff asked.

"Me, too," I said. I checked my watch. Still early. The day had lasted a year, but outdoorsy stuff'll do that.

"I'll show you," said John Raintree. He ambled off into the dark. Tiff squealed and raced after, but I stopped to grab my flashlight.

I didn't turn it on. Half a moon, working toward full, illuminated the night, in a velvet sky so full of stars it looked like dotted swiss.

I inhaled that night smell; the smell of life, of magic, and of danger.

The magic smell quickly changed to an outhouse smell. John Raintree leaned indolently on a tree in the dark, his silhouette crowned with silver moonlight.

Tiff went first. "Oh, my Gawd. It's so dark in here. And smelly. Jeez, do they ever clean this thing?"

"Watch out for the black widows," John called.

Sounds from the pit toilet ceased. The door burst open, and Tiff exploded into the night. She ran toward camp crying, "Ew, ew, ew, oh, god, oh, god, oh, god."

"There aren't really black widows around here, are there?" I asked.

John chuckled. "Highly unlikely. Too high. Too cold. They like deserts, low altitude. Just the same, don't stick your hand under the seat. Want me to wait for you?"

"No, that's okay. Go see if Tiff made it back." I checked under the toilet seat with my flash. No black widows, but a far cry from pleasant. I held my breath, finished as quickly as I could, and stepped out into the clean air. I switched off my light and waited for my night vision to return.

All the little rustlings and scuttling of night creatures going about their business suddenly ceased. A predator? I couldn't remember if bears were nocturnal. Wolves were. Were there wolves here? I walked quickly, and as quietly as I could. Native Americans, I'd read, could walk silently through the forest. How did they do it? I was a blundering ox when I lurched into camp.

"Everything okay?" Chips doused the fire, alone. Everyone else must have gone to bed.

"Yeah, just fine. Tiff get back okay?"

"Yup. Screeching like a banshee." We swapped smiles. "Dived into that tent like the devil was after her. Any idea what happened?"

"Black widow."

"No black widows around here."

"John told her they were in the toilet."

"That John. Always a kidder." Chips smiled.

"Oh, do you know him?"

"Yup. He's my half-brother."

"Is that some sort of secret? I mean you didn't mention it at the campfire."

"Nah. No big thing." I just looked at him. "Sometimes it's better that way." For the first time, Chips didn't try to sound like a cowboy.

I went to bed. I slept, if not the sleep of the just, the sleep of the bone tired, until nearly dawn, when that whispered argument awoke me. Someone was going to tell someone else's boss something. I heard "fraud" and "funding," "criminal charges,"—did someone have a wife? I couldn't make sense of what I heard, and fell back asleep until just after dawn.

I awoke to morning camp sounds and the smell of coffee and wood smoke. My wallet had fallen out of my boot during the night, and my police badge was exposed to view.

As we ate pancakes and eggs, I looked around the fire ring and tried to determine who I had heard in the early hours. No one looked guilty. Even Red seemed chipper and Chips ruffled his hair when he stood to brief us.

Chips finished with, "Okay, folks, we'll pack up and

head out to the next campsite. We go through some beautiful country, but it's going to take us all day, so let's go. If you need help, holler."

I was grateful to see the horses already saddled. Red and John broke camp and loaded the pack horses. We mounted with much less excitement than yesterday, and moved out. I could completely relate to Natalie's keening. "I am so sore! I can't ride this horse for eight more hours. I have to have a ride. Don't you have a jeep or something?" She continued in this vein for several miles.

Bob looked embarrassed and Chips rode farther ahead. John and I were again in the middle, while the college kids rode next, oblivious to everything but each other. Red brought up the rear with the pack animals.

The trail grew steeper, the terrain more primitive, and the heat intense. I had almost emptied my water bottle when Chips raised his right hand like a traffic cop's. We pulled up.

"The trail has a dangerous section up ahead, so I'm going to give you some tips. Horses are sure-footed, but they are not ATVs or mules. They will misstep if you don't give them their heads on this next part." He looked at Natalie. "The trail is narrow. The cliffs go straight up on our right and straight down on our left. If you're nervous, close your eyes, because these horses," he patted Arthur affectionately, "are experienced. They're not going to shy, so just relax and let them take you, and you'll be fine. Any questions?"

Natalie's eyes were huge, and she had a two-handed grip on the saddle horn, reins lax and forgotten on Checkers' neck. John Raintree, unruffled as ever, sat easily in the saddle, a small smile on his lips. The students looked thrilled with the prospect of danger, and Bob Hosley's face was shadowed by his hat as he picked at a mosquito bite on his arm. Red was too far back to see.

Chips put us in order. John Raintree first, followed by Natalie, then himself, Bob, me, the students, and Red last. Red separated the pack horses; if one slipped, he wouldn't lose them all. A sobering thought.

We rode the narrowing trail toward a large rock face, rounded a boulder, and saw half of Colorado spread before us. Way down at the bottom a stream looked small from this height, but it might have been the Colorado river.

One at a time, leaving space between the horses, we traversed the narrow cliff trail our outside feet nearly overhanging the canyon. I trusted Blossom and the trail was solid, but I felt uneasy. I don't like heights. The creak of leather, the drone of insects, the hot smells of horse and sun were hypnotic. The heat beat down on my cowboy hat, and I was glad I had worn it. The danger, although real, seemed remote, and I was caught by surprise when Bob's horse suddenly stopped.

Blossom stumbled as she tried not to bump into Bubbles. I unbalanced toward the cliff, banging my head against solid rock. This tipped my hat off, and it floated away in slow motion. Instinctively I grabbed for it, and slid out of the saddle. Blossom snorted in fear as I clung to the stirrup.

John had made it to the safety of the wider trail ahead; Natalie screamed when she looked back and saw me. John grabbed her reins and hustled her off, followed by Chips. Bob got Bubbles moving again, leaving the trail open ahead of me.

I had no place to put my foot to boost myself up. Blossom braced her feet and rolled her eyes, snorting and huffing. Her sweat-dark coat smelled comfortingly of horse, and I focused on that and clung to the stirrup.

"Hold on, we're coming!"

Blossom's feet scrabbled for purchase, her sides heaving. The saddle slipped sideways, and I saw a partial cut in the girth! I got mad. I prayed the girth would hold and pulled myself up onto the trail, directly under Blossom's belly. She relaxed as my weight stopped pulling her. She dropped her head between her legs and gave me a look that said, "Now what?" I started to laugh, and that was how John and Chips found us when they returned on foot.

"What the hell happened?" Chips hollered.

"I was beginning to think you could ride!" John said.

I tapped Blossom's foreleg and she allowed me to crawl between her feet. I stood at her head, gave her a hug and a kiss, and took up the reins. "Can we continue this somewhere else?" I asked.

Ahead, Natalie and Bob were having a heated discussion that stopped as we approached. "Are you okay?" Natalie gasped.

"What happened back there?" asked Bob.

"Why'd you stop so suddenly?" I asked Bob.

He looked confused. "When?"

"On the trail!"

"Oh. I was uh, uncomfortable and needed to adjust." He looked embarrassed.

"And you picked that spot to do it?"

"Sorry. I'm just glad you're all right." He looked brightly toward the rest of the group as they edged off the dangerous section of trail. "Are we all ready to go on?"

Chips and John exchanged a look. Chips said, "Mount up, folks, we have a long way to go."

The others mounted but I pulled Chips aside. "Someone cut my girth."

"What!" First surprise, then anger crossed his lined face.

"Look." He fingered the slash as I told him what had happened. I watched and waited for his reaction. Did he look guilty?

He scratched under his hat and blew out a breath. "Like I need this," he muttered more to himself than to me. "Why would someone jeopardize you this way?"

"I don't know." I thought about my badge out in the open this morning when I had stuck it into the bottom of my boot last night. At the campfire last night, Chips had told us about the rugged terrain we'd cover today. Everyone knew about the trail, but who knew about my true job? What was going on that was important enough to risk my life? Was I meant to fall to my death or merely to fall out of the saddle and be hurt or scared? Chips looked concerned, but not guilty. "Don't worry, I'm not going to sue." Not unless you're attempting murder.

He smiled. "I appreciate it, but I wasn't worried about that. Who'd be vicious enough to endanger a rider, and a horse, not to mention Greenhorn Trail Rides? Let me check that girth. Looks like it'll hold 'til camp. I can replace it there. Hop up, we've got a way to go."

We stopped for lunch beside a stream and were cautioned not to drink the water. Red distributed sandwiches, chips, fruit and juice. Still no Diet Pepsi. That was going to be on the evaluation. If I didn't get killed.

We lounged in a clearing cooled by shade trees. The

heat outside our glade was unmoving and intense. Jason and Tiff were subdued for once. Natalie leaned against a log near Bob. She took his hand when she saw me watching. His hand lay limply in hers. John, as usual, had found a spot to lie down with his hat over his eyes, and seemed asleep.

An outhouse on a small trailer was provided here. It was an oven inside; the small screens at the top choked with spider webs and insect husks, the smell indescribable. I tried to hurry, but hot jeans on sticky legs didn't cooperate. As I zipped, I heard footsteps. I was about to open the door when two voices spoke.

"How are you doing?" Chips, I thought.

"I'm good. I feel fine." Red.

"Why did you come out here when I told you no?"

"I just . . . " A sigh. "I wanted to."

"I was worried about you, you know? Did you bring your medicine?"

"Yes! I'm not a baby anymore. I can do some things myself." Indignant.

"I know, I'm sorry. I didn't mean it to sound like that. But what if something happens way out here, and the medicine doesn't work? We're miles from a hospital."

"It's under control, Dad." A gasp. "I mean, Chips."

"It's okay. You can call me Dad. You're the son your mom and I never had." He chuckled.

"Yeah. I guess. Um. Can I ask you something?"

"Sure."

"You don't hate me?"

"How could I hate you? It's not your fault your mother took up with a rodeo guy. Besides, you look like her." Chips' voice grew softer. "I loved her once, Red. You know that. But things don't always work out the way we'd like. Hey, we've got each other, right? That's what counts."

"Yeah. I just want to get to know you."

"I want to get to know you, too. You're my son, and that's the way it is." It sounded like they were hugging and crying. I would have hugged somebody too, after that. I sniffled and my eyes and nose ran. It was probably the horrible smell. Chips and Red moved away. Thank God they didn't want to use the toilet.

I burst out of the cubicle like a diver from the depths.

The toasted air felt almost cool. I circled the camp to arrive from another direction.

An extremely crabby, sun-fried bunch of greenhorns pulled up at our second camp late in the afternoon. The camp was in a beautiful meadow near a stream with a small water-fall, a pool for swimming, shade trees, a fabulous mountain view, and a thousand insects per square inch.

I slithered painfully from the saddle, but didn't crumple into a heap this time. The saddle gently released its last bit of girth and thumped to the ground. I had no energy to pick it up. I limped to the water trough with Blossom. She drank long and deep, then raised her head and nuzzled me, long strings of horse spit and water swinging from her muzzle to my shirt. Yum. She meant well, and I kissed her nose and told her she was a good girl, an amazing girl, and the best horse in the world, the way she dug in to keep us both on the cliff trail. "Come on, Blossom." I led her to the make-shift stable for a rub down and horse grub.

The group busied itself with camp-making chores, but much more slowly and quietly than yesterday.

Tiff pushed Jason away saying, "Don't! I'm too hot and sore." Red started a cook fire and laid out supplies. I wanted to help John with the tents, but I flopped against a stack of bedrolls and couldn't force myself to move.

Natalie, the helpless damsel, sprawled ungracefully against the logs surrounding the fire ring. Her visible parts were beet red and her inner thighs, exposed below her short-shorts, looked chafed and raw. Bob ignored her.

Chips went to the ramshackle stable to care for the horses, but when many minutes went by and he didn't emerge, I decided to check. Rising brought tears to my eyes. Every-thing hurt, even my eyelashes.

I convinced myself I could walk the fifty feet to the stable.

"Chips?" The musty smells of hay, manure, and sweaty horses greeted me. Shadowy light revealed several stalls. Tack, leather and tools lined the walls, but the room looked old and unused. Our horses made comforting sounds of chew-ing and hooves shifting—that didn't quite cover the heavy breathing in one stall. I quietly looked in to see Chips lean-ing heavily on Arthur, his head on his arms across the gelding's back. Arthur placidly lipped hay while Chips mumbled and sniffed against him.

"What am I gonna do, huh? That bastard's gonna ruin us, I just know it. Why else did he come here? Money? He already has my design. All I have is the business. Won't even have that if he talks. I can't let him take John down, too."

This made sense if the argument I heard last night was real, and if one of the players was Chips. Somebody thought I was a threat to this big secret. I didn't want to think Chips had slashed my girth. Or any of them; tall, handsome John Raintree, cute and stupid Natalie and doofy Bob from Iowa, for God's sake! The "kids?" Red?

I backed quietly out of the stable and then called, "Hey Chips, you in there? You dead or what?" I counted to ten and shuffled inside.

I found him industriously currying Arthur.

"Hi," I said.

"Hi." He kept his back to me.

"Great ride today. Some beautiful country." Chips set the curry brush on the rim of the stall and Arthur nosed it off. Chips replaced it and Arthur did it again. This was clearly a game and after three rounds, Chips fed Arthur a wilted-looking carrot, then with a final pat, latched the stall door. He seemed cheerful as he set the curry brush on a shelf.

"So, things going okay?" I ventured as we left the stable.

"Yeah, sure. Except for the girth today."

"I have a theory about that. Want to hear it?"

"Sure," he said without enthusiasm.

"Okay. I'm not necessarily the target. It could have been any of your riders. Business sabotage. What do you think?"

He didn't respond, but led me to a clear stream, with wonderful warm boulders to perch on. We did.

He looked at me. "I'm sorry, but I'm sure you know someone went through your stuff last night. It was me."

One mystery solved, and no, the great detective didn't know my "stuff" had been gone through. Only my wallet.

"I'll tell you something—because I don't know what else to do." He sighed. "I'm being blackmailed. I'm to keep quiet, or I'll lose Greenhorn Trail Rides."

"I thought you just worked here?"

"I'm a silent partner."

"What are you supposed to keep quiet about?"

"In the off-season I design software, freelance. I sent my first project to a company last year. It was stupid not to patent it first, but I was confident the company would purchase it. I was told the design was out of date, not practical, etc. Then, this year, the design was marketed by a different company. I went back to the company I sent it to, and of course, they know nothing about my proposal. I threatened to make a stink. They threatened lawsuit. Then I got an anonymous letter, I'm sure from the person who stole my design, saying I'd lose the ranch business if I pursued a lawsuit."

"Well," I said. I was thoroughly confused.

"I know you must think I'm an idiot, but maybe you could give me some advice? I can't talk to anyone officially until I know more."

"Is John involved?"

"Yes, but I'm trying to protect him. There are special circumstances surrounding the ranch's ownership. The blackmailer can never own the ranch. Either the blackmailer doesn't know that, and really wants the ranch, or he does know and doesn't care—just wants to make sure I won't sue."

"Can I ask you something?"

"Sure." He slid off the boulder, offering me his callused hand.

"Is Red sick?"

"Epilepsy."

"Is Red involved in this mess with the business?" He didn't answer, but walked stiff-legged toward camp.

"He's your son, right?"

He was in my face so fast I didn't have time to back up. "Red is not involved, was never involved, and will never be involved. Got it?" His sweaty face was inches from mine, and he had changed from worried blackmail victim to snarling lion in milliseconds.

My reply was forestalled by a piercing scream. We hauled ass back to camp to find the group huddled near one of the tents, where blue-jeaned legs protruded, absolutely still, and an ominous rattle echoed within.

I did a quick head-count. It was Jason in the tent. John muttered calming phrases that didn't help. Tiff held herself and cried. Bob had his arms around Natalie who craned her neck for a better look. Red held a long stick, but didn't move. I glanced into the tent. Big snake.

I hate snakes worse than a four car pile-up on Santa Monica Boulevard.

Jason didn't move. Either he'd fainted or the snake had got him. The snake kept rattling.

Chips took over at once. Red handed him the stick and Chips gently pulled back the tent flap. The snake was huge, and lay coiled on Jason's stomach, facing us.

John moved us away from the tent. The snake stopped rattling. I could smell the cook fire and an odor of burned beans. No one moved. Shadows had gathered in the camp and I realized how dark it had become. Jason moaned and the snake rattled a little. Chips was almost in the tent, the stick closer to the snake. A month passed and no one moved or breathed. Suddenly, Chips backed out of the tent and turned, the rattler draped over the end of his stick. It was a monster with a huge, bulging belly. Two feet plus dangled on each side of the branch.

Chips strode away toward the outhouse trail. No way would I use the bathroom for the rest of the trip. Even if I exploded.

John and I squashed into the small tent. At Jason's head I checked his pulse and breathing. He seemed extremely hot, but his respiration was strong. John examined the bite marks on Jason's right hand and left thigh.

"How is he? Is he going to be okay?" I asked.

"He's fine."

"He's not fine. You guys must have a snakebite kit, right? Do something!" The fang marks gave me the willies, like two little vampire attacks.

"If any venom is in those bites, it's such a small amount, and he's such a big guy, he might feel a little sick, but it's not going to kill him." When John said it like that, something clicked. "That snake didn't crawl in here by itself," he went on. "It had just fed. With a bulge like that in its middle, it wouldn't crawl around a camp full of noisy people in daylight. And Jason's lucky it was full grown."

"How is it lucky to be bit by the biggest snake in Colorado?"

"A baby rattler dumps all its venom at once, because it

hasn't learned to use it yet. A big old snake like that one," he nodded at the bites, "only injects enough venom to kill whatever it's going to eat, and it knew Jason was too big to eat. Looks like it struck out of fear, and didn't inject much venom. I'll watch him for a while, make sure he doesn't go into shock, but I think he's going to be fine."

Red came to the tent flap and handed in the first aid kit. John started to swab and bandage the bites.

I asked John, "Are you scared of snakes?" Smooth.

"I respect snakes. Our culture believes snakes are sacred."

"What culture is that?"

He grunted. "Navajo. Dineh." He smoothed the bandages and stood, not even creaking or cracking. I backed out of the tent and he followed.

"You're Navajo?"

"Half."

"Were you raised Navajo? On a reservation?"

"Yes." He didn't want to discuss this, which made me want to, but I let it drop.

Outside the tent, the others milled about, hashing it over.

"What happened?" Bob Hosley asked.

"I don't know!" said Tiff. "I asked Jason to get my book for me, I wanted to show him something, and he went toward the tents. I heard him shout—but it sounded so strange. When he didn't come back, I went to check." She dissolved into tears.

Bob said, "Yes, Natalie and I went for a walk, and when we got back. . ."

Natalie added, "I was going to lie down for a while in my tent. I don't have much stamina, you know." We all knew more about Natalie than we wanted to. "I don't know how Bob does it! He's just so athletic." She glanced at "athletic Bob" and his little potbelly, fleshy appendages and myopic gaze. "Anyway, when we got back, Jason was lying in my tent with that snake!" She made it sound like a tryst.

"This is your tent?" I asked.

Natalie's round eyes grew even rounder. "Yes!" she squeaked. "I was going to lie down. I would have been bitten!

Red thrust a burned bean pot at me and said, "I need

this. Would you go wash it in the stream?"

I obediently went to the stream. I had no detergent, but supposed that was best for the stream. I squatted behind a tumble of boulders and tried to scrub off the carbonized beans with rocks and sand, but it didn't work like in the movies.

I heard people approaching. I was about to stand and hail them, when I realized they were arguing. I lurked.

"I've just about had it Bob!" Natalie. "I guess you thought this romantic little adventure would rekindle our marriage, but it's not working. You know my idea of roughing it is a hotel without twenty-four hour room service! And you haven't kept your word. If you don't, I'll do it for you. Look at me! I'm sunburned, mosquito-bitten, starving to death on this camp food, and now a snake in my tent!"

"Now, Natalie, we agreed to try, right?" Bob, placating.

"I don't want to try! I am not a good sport! I don't know why I married you. You are a spineless, dishonest worm. I won't support your wild schemes any more. No more of my inheritance is going into your software or any of your other ideas, for that matter."

"But Natalie, just a little longer. We can make things work."

"No! I'm tired and dirty and done! I married a thief! My mother is rolling over in her grave. I let you drag me out here into the middle of nowhere so you could come clean, and you haven't. After this stupid horse thing, I'm checking into the Denver Hilton. Then, I'll file for divorce. I don't believe you ever loved me. I was just a sex-toy with money!" I heard Natalie stomp off toward camp. Bob stayed, and I was stuck. I was afraid to move because the scree would surely make a noise.

My thigh cramped. My hip hurt. I wanted to eat. Red needed the bean pot. I was about to scream and confess my really bad manners when Bob sighed and slid off the boulder. It sounded like he threw something—a small rock?—into the stream. Just as I was ready to die, his footsteps moved away. I creaked upright, and took the pot back to Red.

Complete darkness enveloped us as we ate. No fireside banter tonight. Jason joined us for dinner, complimented the chef, thanked his rescuers. No one else moved or spoke. We left the camp a mess and went to bed, too spent to bother.

Panicked voices, footsteps and a bobbing flashlight beam dragged me from a dreamless sleep. I threw off my sleeping bag and yanked on my boots. My watch said a little after four. I hustled toward the noise and added my own beam to the scene at Natalie's tent. Bob, in tears, knelt by Natalie, who lay still and silent in her sleeping bag.

"We had a fight. I felt bad," Bob was saying. "I just wanted to make up. I came over to talk and she was gone. Gone!" He patted and smoothed the sleeping bag. John, already in the tent, shook his head in the classic television manner to indicated that Natalie was dead. The gesture didn't seem funny in real life. Chips urged Bob from the tent, then gave his head a quick jerk to indicate he wanted me to check things out. No problem. That was my intention. I beckoned to John.

"Get everyone back to bed," I told him. "Tell them there's nothing they can do, and ask them to stay in their tents." John nodded.

The others, in various states of dress, looked shocked, eyes large in the artificial light. Red's hair stood straight up and his freckles were bright on his pale face.

I got my camera, stood in the tent opening, and took pictures. Everything was neat, precisely in its place. Natalie's boots sat side by side along the far wall of the tent. Her travel packs were zipped, her personal belongings out of sight. Not even a water bottle. The floor of the tent was suprisingly clean. I knelt next to her body. Her pale skin, the circulation gone, had a waxy sheen. Her eyes and mouth were slightly open. One arm was tucked inside the sleeping bag, the other out where John had felt for a pulse. Her bag zipped to her armpits. I eyed the bottom of the sleeping bag, not discounting another snake. No movement. I gently ran my flash up and down the bag, just in case. No wriggling or rattling. More pictures. I carefully unzipped the bag and studied the body. No obvious trauma, no bites, stab wounds, nothing to indicate how she died. I took another picture. I wanted to preserve the scene, in case it was a scene.

We had no cell phone, to my knowledge, and I cursed my stubborn determination to be "off-line" for the weekend. I would check. No one could leave camp to get help until daylight. Too dangerous to travel this country in the dark. If

Natalie had been murdered, we all might be in danger.

Of course I suspected Bob, the spouse, always the prime suspect. Still, their argument by the stream could have been nothing more than an irate Natalie throwing out unfounded accusations. She was overweight and overwrought. What if she had simply died? Then again, it had sounded like Bob had a lot to lose if Natalie divorced him. If she died, he might inherit a substantial sum.

Greenhorn Trail Rides had some problems. Was that related? I didn't see how, but our ratio of disaster and drama on a three day trek seemed high for a group of eight. I checked Natalie's bags. Nothing unusual. Then I saw a box of tampons. If I wanted to hide something from a man, particularly my husband, that's where I'd put it.

At the bottom of Natalie's box I found a Medic-Alert bracelet. The flip side read, Heart Condition.

"So." Bob hovered over me. I turned and saw a fist-sized rock in his hand. "You know."

"Know what?" Brilliant rejoinder. He stood close above me.

"Don't pretend you don't know."

I dropped the medical bracelet. "I know Natalie had a heart condition. Why did she hide it?" I meant, why did you hide it?

"She was vain. She didn't want anyone to think she was less than perfect."

"And she wasn't?" I scooted back a little.

"She wanted a divorce. I didn't want it. I loved her." He snorted a creepy laugh. "Maybe love isn't the word. I needed her."

"Needed her money, more like."

His gaze sharpened. "What do you know about that?" When I didn't respond, he said, "I see. Get up." I didn't move. He grabbed my hair and said, "If you scream, it's all over, right here, right now. Get up." He swept up Natalie's bracelet and used my hair to force me up, then pushed me out of the tent, his fist twisted into the back of my sweatshirt collar, choking me.

Chips lay by the fire ring; too still. I prayed he was breathing, but couldn't tell. Where was John? And everyone else?

"It's time for another accident." Great. Bob's flashlight

did a poor job of lighting the footpath toward the outhouse. Of course. I would probably die there.

"So," I yelped, "explain to me why Natalie had to go. Was it only the money?"

"Shut up."

I remembered the conversation I'd overheard the first night. It made sense if one of the people was Bob. And, maybe Chips? Chips had seemed worried about the ranch. Was Bob a blackmailer and a murderer? Natalie had called him a thief down by the stream.

"Why do you have to be so nosy? Everything was going so well. I was getting money, and having fun lording it over people. But no. First Natalie, then Chips, then you."

"I don't get it. First Natalie what?"

"Don't be stupid. You know she was going to tell Chips that I stole his software design and was blackmailing him. She was going to divorce me because she wanted an honest man. Christ. First she wants a rich man, then an honest man." He ran a hand through his thinning hair. I didn't think Natalie's requests were all that unreasonable. "That's why we came out here. Natalie thought I would come clean with Chips, to appease her. I had something else in mind."

"What?"

"I could take his precious little ranch away if he spilled. He wasn't going to talk."

"What would you do with a ranch?"

"Jeez, you're dense." It wasn't the first time I'd been told that. He yelled, "I didn't want the ranch! I just wanted Chips to think I did, so I could go on with my life. Now do you get it?" Flecks of spit collected at the corners of his mouth.

"So, you put a snake in her tent? Tried to kill her?"

"Snake? Of course not. I hate snakes." He shuddered.

"Well, why'd you kill Natalie?" Let's get it out on the table.

He crumpled into tears. "Don't! Don't you say that. I didn't kill her. We could have worked it out. She wouldn't really have told them! It's just she's not . . . she's not an outdoor person."

"So you killed her by accident?"

"No! Get it through your stupid head!" He waved the

rock. If I lunged, would a broken shoulder be worse or better than a broken head?

"I didn't kill her! We had years ahead of us! I'm not sure, but I think one reason Natalie was so grumpy was because she was pregnant! I wouldn't kill my own child."

No, Natalie was just a bitch. The box of tampons probably precluded a pregnancy. See, men never look. They don't want to know these things.

"Okay, okay. You didn't kill her. Why did you cut my girth?"

"What's a girth?"

"You know, the thing you cut under my saddle. When I almost fell off into a forty mile deep canyon?"

"I didn't do that. Why are you accusing me of all these things? I wanted money. I didn't try to kill anybody. What is wrong with you?"

Oh, I don't know. I guess I'm just unreasonable. "Would you just back up a minute so I can stand? I'm getting a cramp." Amazingly, he did. I rose. He dropped the rock.

"Is that blood on the rock?" I asked. "Did you hit Chips?"

"Yes, but just a little. He's fine. I wanted to talk to you. I need some help.

"What kind of help?"

"You're in PR, right? I need to market my new software design, and I need some ideas. Now that Natalie's gone, I'll have to do it on my own."

Great. A total wacko with delusions of innocence and a future career.

"You threw something into the stream earlier—what was it?"

He looked sad. "Oh. My wedding ring. I guess now it's really over."

I didn't know if he meant the trail ride, his marriage, or his future. He wandered away into the dark, and I stood there, heart pounding, wondering what to do next. "If you didn't do it, who did?" I shouted after him. "I'll find out you know. I'm not going to give up."

"I know." A rich voice from the blackness. John Raintree stepped into the circle of moonlight and my stomach fell a couple of feet. I felt light-headed as all my speculation clicked into place. My saddle. My badge. Chips had looked through my stuff, and of course he told his brother and business partner I was a cop. If I had an accident, my natural curiosity, and my blossoming personal connection to Chips would be severed.

Snakes. John said his culture revered snakes. No problem to find a nice big one and hide it. Except Jason got bitten, not me, and Natalie died but not, apparently, from snakebite.

"Tell me why you chose a well-fed, almost harmless snake? And why Jason?"

John stood arm's length away, relaxed and handsome as ever. His expression said it all. He knew I knew.

"I didn't choose it. I just didn't have time to find the perfect snake. The snake was supposed to bite Natalie. Induce a heart-attack."

"You knew she had a heart-condition? How? She hid it."

"She put it on her application for the ride. We do have insurance requirements. She was a vain, nasty woman."

I nodded.

"I also found her Medic Alert bracelet in her bag the first night. Just like I found your badge."

So much for my thought that a man wouldn't open a box of tampons.

"Why did you kill her?"

"Natalie had to die so Bob would take the blame. Chips has worked hard all his life. At least I had the Reservation. Chips had nothing except Red and the horses. Technically, the ranch is mine. That's the problem."

"Chips designs software, right? You can make a good living at that. Why is this all so despairing?"

"Chips designed one program. That's it. But it's brilliant. He didn't, and doesn't know what he's doing. He sent it to Bob Hosley's company. Hosley is in new design and acquisition. When Chips' design came in, with no patent, no record, Bob snatched it up. He intercepted all further communication and patented and sold it as his own. He didn't get as much for it as he would have on the open market, because he worked for the company, so he started to blackmail Chips. His first mistake was that he told his wife. He wanted to be the big man in her eyes, but it backfired. His second mistake was not knowing that Chips would tell me. I am the one he should have worried about."

"I'm still a little lost. If he stole the design from Chips, what was there for him to blackmail Chips about? Shouldn't it be the other way around?"

John smiled and ran a finger down my arm. Even through my sweatshirt, I felt a chill. His eyes glowed black and his silver hair flowed away from his Navajo features. He looked so wild at this moment; my primitive reaction was almost my undoing.

"Oh," I breathed. "The Reservation. The Council. This has to do with tribal funding. Chips can't be involved in Greenhorn Trailrides except as an employee." That was the part about having to return money and the probable disgrace both men would face not only in the small community, but also in Navajo culture.

John took my hand like a lover, and it all made terrible sense. The attempts on my life, and the clever frame of Bob for Natalie's death.

"How did you kill her?" I needed to know.

"I got rid of her heart medicine, and then gave her a thrill." His teeth reflected moonlight in a feral smile. My scalp contracted as he pulled me toward the outhouse.

"This will be perfectly understandable," he said conversationally as we walked hand in hand. "You got up to use the outhouse and were snakebit. It does happen. Rattlers get into the outhouses at night because they're warm. Normally, we have a rubber seal on the bottom of the door to prevent that, but this one came loose."

He reached for the door of the toilet, pulling me in front of him by the hand. As he opened the door, I grabbed him and swung him around so he was off balance and went in first. He still had my hand. I heard the rattles of many tails as he fell over the raised step. He screamed and thrashed, my hand a strange connection. I pulled back and he lunged out, then fell. I slammed the door on a thousand maracas.

John's eyes glazed, his hand went lax in mine. Our physical contact remained unbroken. My tears dripped onto his face as I knelt beside him and watched his life drain away. My screams roused the camp.

John Raintree died from the bites of half a dozen baby

rattlers. Bob was indicted for blackmail, grand theft—because the software design turned out to be a million dollar winner—and attempted murder. Strangely enough, no one could prove Natalie's death had been caused by anything but too much stress and not enough nitro. Chips paid back the tribal funds, making it a donation in his brother's name. Not because the council had asked, or even known about Chips' involvement in the business.

I still love horses, but have decided to postpone getting one of my own. I figure I've already had the ride of a lifetime.

Victoria Heckman:

Victoria Heckman is the award winning author of the "K.O.'d in . . ." Hawaii mystery series. *K.O.'d in Honolulu* is available in paperback, CD and download from Writers Exchange E Publishing <www.writers-exchange.com/epublishing/>. *K.O.'d in the Volcano* is due out in early 2002. She is working on the third book, *K.O.'d in Hawaiian Sovereignty*. She has also published over sixty short stories and articles.

Victoria is President of the Central Coast Chapter of Sisters in Crime and a member of Sisters in Crime National's E Publishing Committee and the Police Writers Association. Her website: www.victoriaheckman.com

THE BLACK HAWTHORNE

by Carolyn Wheat

I love cats. And I like to help my friends, so when Mrs. Simpson-Phelps, my next-door neighbor, asked me to cat-sit for her, what could I say but yes? Little did I know that the job would entail the skills of a private detective—which I most decidedly am not, though I do read what my husband refers to as "those stupid mysteries."

I know her cats. Everyone in our Georgetown neighborhood knows her cats. We see the curious Tigger in her backyard, acting like his Winnie-the-Pooh namesake, all stripes and bounces, peeking under the fence, jumping at squirrels. We see Paddington, the Fred Astaire of cats, graceful, slender, impeccably dressed in a sleek black fur tuxedo with a white patch at his throat, walking along the back fence, delicately stepping over each picket. We see Arthur, the Mighty Hunter, stalk through the tall summer grass, on the prowl for a mouse, a bird, anything he can capture and crow over. Once he "caught" a charcoal briquette from my barbecue, and meowed as loudly and as proudly as if it had been the biggest rat in the world.

You have to be a very close neighbor of Mrs. Simpson-Phelps to see her fourth cat. Little Orphan Annie, who's very shy, likes nothing better than to bask in the sun, preferably on a self-made cushion of newspaper or a grocery bag. She views the world through grass-green eyes that see everything and register surprise at nothing.

Mrs. Simpson-Phelps and her feline family welcomed me to the neighborhood when I first moved in three years ago. I was a newlywed, she newly widowed. We started chatting over the back fence, the way neighbors do, and soon I was picking up one or the other of her straying pets and handing him over the fence. She handed me homemade scones, perfectly toasted crumpets dripping real butter, lemon-curd tarts—all the delicacies of her native England.

Mrs. Simpson-Phelps was Violet Simpson of London's East End till she met a handsome GI named Harry Phelps and became a war bride. Now she wanted to go home again. But what to do about the cats? That was where I came in.

". . . just couldn't trust an agency, so impersonal. And my dear niece, Wanda, lives all the way in Fredericksburg, so it won't do to ask her, though I know she'd oblige if she could. She's a doctor, you know, very busy. She suggested I board them with a vet, but I can't bear to think . . ."

"Of course I'll take care of them, Mrs. Simpson-Phelps," I said warmly. I'd said it once already, but my neighbor's anxiety about leaving her pets seemed to have affected her hearing. After all, I reasoned—already mentally making my case to Bud, my skeptical husband, who would no doubt call me a pushover—how hard could it be? I'd open cat food cans, empty the litter pan, let them sit on my lap and purr for a while, and that would be that. Just because Bud called our neighbor's cats The Wild Bunch didn't mean they were really . . .

"NO, Arthur, Mrs. Simpson-Phelps said firmly, as Arthur made a gigantic leap into the air, going after a low-flying blue jay. Arthur plopped down on the brick patio and licked his white paw furiously, as if to show he had no interest whatsoever in creatures of the avian persuasion.

We were in our usual conversational mode: standing on either side of the whitewashed fence that separated our tiny backyards. Around us, forming a square, were the rear entrances of townhouses, their warm Georgian brick lit by early spring sun. My apricot tree was in full creamy bloom; Mrs. Simpson-Phelps's weeping cherry was just budding in pink.

"I'm so pleased, Nikki. Thanks ever so, love. With you looking after them, I know my darlings will be in good hands." She clasped her own beringed hands to her breast.

Mrs. Simpson-Phelps had one of the few clotheslines left in our rapidly gentrifying neighborhood. She did her own hand washing and often hung lace dresser scarves and linen tea towels out to dry in the sun, proclaiming electric dryers the ruin of good Irish linen. I noticed a clothespin dangling from the line; whatever it had secured had fallen to the ground.

"Look, I think Annie has..." I began, but my neighbor had already noticed; she made a beeline for the white-and-tabby cat. Annie was busily kneading the tea-towel into a cushion, getting it ready for her plump little body.

"Annie, love, please give me that nice clean towel," my neighbor cooed, deftly pulling the now-dirty scrap of linen from under the cat's white feet. Annie meowed indignantly and stalked, tail high, into the house through the open French doors.

"Oh, dear." Mrs. Simpson-Phelps looked at me ruefully. "They are rather a handful, aren't they?"

I was beginning to have second thoughts about cat-sitting The Wild Bunch, so I changed the subject. "When was the last time you were in England?" I asked.

"Oh, not for years and years. I believe little Prince Charles was just being christened the last time I was home. Oh, dear, I shall have forgotten everything I ever knew about getting round London, I know I shall."

"But why haven't you gone back?" I asked, my head filled with romantic stories about her family cutting her off with a shilling because she dared to marry an American soldier.

"Because of my kitties, of course. England has the MOST barbaric quarantine laws, and I just couldn't bear to leave my darlings home for so long." Mrs. Simpson-Phelps gazed fondly at Paddington, who glided along the back fence with the graceful balance of a tightrope walker.

"Before I had this lot, there were other cats in my life," she explained. "Let me see—there was Bunny Brown and his sister Sue, Alice in Wonderland—she was a sweet little thing, pure white and deaf as a post. And Mole and Ratty and Mr. Toad—the fattest ginger tom you ever did see. I never could bear to part with them, or to have them quarantined for six whole months. But now," she said, her face clouding, "with my sister Mavis ill, I really must go over. No more excuses."

"Oh," I said. I explained my melodramatic picture of family opposition to her American husband, and she laughed.

"No, it was nothing like that, love." Her chuckle was as rich as Devonshire cream. "My family adored Harry, really they did. The only thing my father wanted was that I keep the family name, which is why I go by Simpson-Phelps. As though my old dad was a duke instead of a pubkeeper. In return, he gave us The Black Hawthorne as a wedding present."

She said the words in capital letters. I had to ask what The Black Hawthorne was, and she responded by inviting me to "come round at once and be educated."

It was my first entry into my neighbor's house. For all our good-natured back-fence chatting, we had never been inside one another's homes. I had to admit I was curious; it's always instructive to see how others choose to live.

When she opened her front door to let me in, Tigger bounced at me and twined himself around my legs, mewing pitifully. "Shush, you awful Tig," my neighbor said, her voice tinged with a mixture of mock annoyance and shameless indulgence. "You'll have Nikki thinking I never feed you, when the fact is you're positively stuffed with tinned mackerel."

The front parlor—Georgetown houses have front and back parlors instead of living rooms—was a little piece of England tucked away in the capitol of the colonies. A Victorian sofa of hideous proportions occupied the place of honor across from the fireplace, and vases of dried weeds with peacock feather accents sat in corners on dark, carved tables with marble tops. The walls were festooned with family photographs in oval frames, along with pallid watercolors.

"There," my hostess said proudly, pointing to the mantel, "that's The Black Hawthorne."

I had no trouble seeing why she spoke so respectfully of her heirloom. It was a Chinese ginger jar, slightly taller than a cat, of a deep rich black with a twisted-tree design on it. Very graceful, very old, very valuable.

"The Black Hawthorne was brought from China by Captain Hosea Simpson in 1869," my hostess explained. "My nephew, Gerry, says it's worth a small fortune, though it is only Ch'ing instead of Ming. Whatever that means," she added with a laugh.

"Such a shame I shall be going to England just when Gerry is visiting over here, but it can't be helped."

The words burst out of me before I could stop myself. "But Mrs. Simpson-Phelps, Violet, you can't just leave a thing like that on an open mantel! What about the cats? Don't you worry that one of them will—"

"Nonsense, Nikki," my neighbor said complacently. "My darlings know how important The Black Hawthorne is to me. They would never knock it down. Would you, pets?" Since only Annie was in the room, sitting this time on a real cushion, the objet d'art, perched on the mantel with the Toby jugs and the seashell-statue that said "Souvenir of Brighton 1943" was probably safe, at least for the moment. Wherever Tigger had disappeared to, his temporary absence gave the precious object a reprieve.

I stayed long enough to drink what Mrs. Simpson-Phelps proudly called "a proper cup of tea" and to eat two of her melt-in-the-mouth scones. Just as I was finishing the last few crumbs, Tigger bounced back into the room, dragging a shopping bag after him. I laughed as he shook his head from side to side, trying to free himself from the handle, which had wrapped itself around his neck.

"Nikki, it isn't a bit funny," my neighbor scolded as she caught Tigger and lifted the twine handle over his head while the cat squirmed and squealed with fright. "He might strangle on one of these carry bags. I should never have them in the house. And before I go, I intend to get rid of every one I have, even the lovely Christmas ones from Lord and Taylor's."

I apologized for laughing and promised once again to take good care of The Wild Bunch. I eyed The Black Hawthorne on my way out of the parlor. One more thing to worry about during the three weeks Mrs. Simpson-Phelps would be away. I wasn't just a cat-sitter any more; I was a ginger jar-sitter as well.

Still, The Black Hawthorne had survived The Wild Bunch and their predecessors for lo these many years; why should three more weeks put it in danger?

I put the ginger jar and my neighbor out of mind for the next week. It was getting closer and closer to April 15, when my office, the dreaded Internal Revenue Service, would be swamped with last-minute tax returns. I worked late every night and so waited till the last minute to shop for a birthday present for my sister in St. Louis. On my lunch hour, I crossed Constitution Avenue to the massive gift shop at the Smithsonian's Museum of American History. That's the home of the real ruby slippers and has more gift ideas than a whole raft of catalogues. Acres and acres of everything from replicas of Egyptian gold earrings to place mats with American advertising logos. Paper dolls of the First Ladies and Japanese playing cards. Rice-paper kites and Civil War soldiers and scarves with stained glass designs and dominoes with pictures of Presidents and make-it-yourself cardboard White Houses—and that's just the first floor.

The ginger jar sat on a glass shelf along with marble bookends in the form of lions. "Reproduction Ch'ing Dynasty ginger jar in unusual black lacquer with hawthorne pattern," the printed label read. "While primarily produced for the export market," it burbled, "these vases are among the rarest of their period. Add a touch of Oriental elegance to YOUR home with this reproduction of the real thing."

I bought Susan a silk scarf with purple irises and a silver iris scarf-pin. But I couldn't get the ginger jar out of my mind; its image followed me onto the bus for the ride home to Georgetown. Had Mrs. Simpson-Phelps made up the story about her sea-captain forbear, passing off a museum reproduction as a valuable antique? Did that explain her willingness to leave the ginger jar within easy reach of feline tails, or did she really own the genuine article—and have an extraordinary faith in the kindness of cats?

Either way, the ginger jar would become my responsibility in the morning. Should I leave it in its place of honor on my neighbor's mantel, or should I take it to my own home for safekeeping while she was away? I pondered both sides of the question as the bus made its way into the picturesque narrow streets of Georgetown. I continued thinking about it as I walked along the brick sidewalk toward my town house.

I had no clear answer as I rang the next-door bell the next day. I found Mrs. Simpson-Phelps in a state of pre-travel panic. "Oh dear, where IS my passport?" she asked, rummaging through a kitchen drawer. "Do you think I've bought enough cat food, love?" She pointed to a mountain of canned gourmet meals for felines.

I never had a chance to say yes. "And on top of everything, Gerry and Wanda—Harry's brother's oldest girl—have been quarreling over The Black Hawthorne. They've each asked me to leave it to them in my will. As if I could think about something as trivial as a will at a time like this!"

She was putting her hat on as we spoke, but that didn't stop her telling me, for the fifth time since asking me to cat-sit, how Annie hated liver but Paddy doted on it and how Arthur was not under any circumstances to be allowed outside.

"I'd worry myself sick thinking he might be lost, you see," she explained. "Which reminds me. At least Wanda has some appreciation of my feelings. She promised to take good care of my darlings if anything ever happened to me. In return for The Black Hawthorne, no doubt. But that's more than Gerry offered. He can't stand cats, made no bones about it when he came to see me. 'Keep them away from me, Aunt Violet,' he begged. 'Especially that black one!' As if my Paddy wasn't the gentlest creature alive," she finished indignantly.

The doorbell rang. I went to open it, since my neighbor was proving her point by cuddling the black cat, murmuring endearments into his oversized ears.

The woman at the door was about my age, tall, with blonde hair cut short and sculpted to her head like a cap. A Valkyrie with a Vidal Sassoon haircut. "I'm Wanda Phelps," she explained, offering me a hand to shake. The other hand held a handsome wine-colored doctor's bag.

"I'm driving Aunt Violet to the airport," she said. Ms. Phelps looked meaningfully at her aunt as she added, "I'll probably pop in on the weekends to see that everything's all right. I see patients at a free clinic on Saturdays and it's on my way. But I couldn't make the trip every day, so I'm really glad you're taking care of her cats."

"Oh, it's no trouble," I said lightly, noting that Tigger was about to make a giant leap from the back of the sofa to the top of the china closet. Arthur stood at the French doors, meowing to be let out into the sunny summer day.

Mrs. Simpson-Phelps put Paddy down and stroked Annie's white fur. "Oh, I must go, mustn't I?" she asked Wanda in a plaintive tone.

Turning to me, she said, "Here are the keys. DO pet them

for me, will you?" Her eyes filled with tears.

"Yes, of course I will," I said, impulsively grasping her plump hand in mine and giving it a farewell squeeze.

It's hard to leave your children in someone else's hands.

As the door closed behind Wanda's hand-knit pink sweater and Mrs. Simpson-Phelps's good traveling hat, I looked at The Wild Bunch and said, "It's up to you, guys. You can be good kitties or you can break an old lady's heart. Which is it going to be?"

Despite the full bowls of food on the kitchen floor, all four felines ran to the mountain of cat food cans and begged as though they hadn't eaten in a week. I sighed.

Nevertheless, the three weeks my neighbor was gone passed smoothly. I opened can after can of gourmet cat food, cooked liver for Paddy, changed litter box after litter box, picked up hairballs, and generally made sure things were all right in the Simpson-Phelps menagerie. Each Saturday morning Dr. Wanda Phelps's white Volvo pulled into a parking space on our narrow street and the tall blonde navigated the cobblestones, her wine-colored medical bag in her hand.

The day before Mrs. Simpson-Phelps was due to arrive home from her native land, I opened the door to chaos. I looked first at Paddington, perched on the mantel licking his paw. Then I saw what lay on the floor beneath him. I looked at Arthur, batting something around the floor while Tigger poked his head out from inside a shopping bag with twine handles. Finally, I looked at Annie, curled up on a bundle of pink stuff she'd managed to knead into a cushion.

Any other cat-sitter would have gotten out the broom and cleaned up the mess.

I called the police.

"Just what is it you think happened here?" the stalwart, skeptical, just-the-facts-ma'am detective—who also happened to be my husband—asked for the third time.

I took a deep breath and started in again. "Bud, I've already told you. We're supposed to think Paddy broke The Black Hawthorne," I explained. "When I came in, he was on the mantel, licking his paw. And, as you can see, the jar's in pieces on the floor."

My hand waved at the shards of black lacquered porcelain that lay on the parquet. "But Paddy's the most graceful cat I've ever seen. There's no way he would have been clumsy enough to knock that thing down."

Detective Bud Parker raised a single eyebrow. Apparently the gracefulness of cats didn't qualify as admissible evidence.

"If your men do a thorough examination of the mantelpiece," I went on, "I think they'll find traces of liver. Cooked liver that someone put up there to lure Paddy onto the mantel."

Now the other eyebrow went up. I'd seen this expression before, and it did not denote acquiescence to my point of view.

"Liver," he said. He signed. "Was this on MURDER SHE WROTE or something?"

"And then there's Tigger," I said, ignoring the comment. The fact that the hour between 8 and 9 P.M. on Sunday evening was as sacred to me as the Super Bowl was to him had no bearing on the facts at hand.

I pointed to the colorful shopping bag with the dangerous twine handles Mrs. Simpson-Phelps had been so concerned about. "It's from Harrod's. That's in London," I added helpfully. "A place our neighbor hasn't visited in donkey's years. Which means that someone who HAD been in London recently came and left it here. What's more," I said, going for the clincher, "I know Mrs. Simpson-Phelps got rid of all her shopping bags because she was afraid Tigger would get his head caught in the handles. So that bag was brought here while she was away."

I sat back on the velvet-covered sofa, which was just as uncomfortable as it looked, waiting for Bud to catch up with my thinking. "Mrs. Simpson-Phelps has a nephew who lives in England. He's here in Washington right now—and he had his eye on his aunt's valuable antique."

Bud nodded. His eyebrows were back in their normal position; he was clearly more comfortable discussing human rather than feline psychology.

"Look at Annie," I continued, pointing to where the green-eyed cat sat in sphinx pose on a hand-knitted pink sweater. Even the arrival of several heavy-footed police officers hadn't moved her from her comfortable seat.

"See what she's sitting on?" Without waiting for an answer, I went on. "I last saw that sweater on Wanda, Mrs. Simpson-Phelps's niece. You remember, I met her just before Mrs. Simpson-Phelps left. And she had designs on the vase, too. That's why she came every Saturday, to show her aunt how much she cares for the cats, so Mrs. Simpson-Phelps will leave her the ginger jar in her will."

"So you think Wanda is behind all this?" Bud asked. "You've seen her enter the house; the pink sweater is hers—maybe she tried to steal the vase and broke it instead."

"No," I answered. "It was Gerry who stole the real vase. Then he broke this reproduction so his aunt would think it was destroyed forever."

"How do you know it was him instead of the niece?"

"Because of Arthur," I replied.

"Arthur? Who's he?" Bud demanded. "Another nephew?"

I laughed, then pointed at the gunmetal gray cat with the white peninsula on his clown face. "That's Arthur," I said. "And if you'll look at what he has between his paws, you'll see what I mean about Gerry."

Bud hoisted his bulk out of the blue velvet sofa—which clung to its sitters like the sea to its dead—and walked to where Arthur guarded his captured prey. "Hey," he said, picking up the object, "this is a charcoal briquette. What's this cat doing with—"

"That's what I mean," I said triumphantly. "Arthur's been outside. Mrs. Simpson-Phelps specifically told me he wasn't to go out while she was away. Somebody disobeyed her and let him out. You remember the Adzakian's barbecue last Sunday—Arthur must have captured a briquette from their grill."

"So why couldn't Wanda—"

"Because she loved the cats," I said triumphantly. "She wouldn't have let Arthur go outside. And she'd never have left a shopping bag where Tigger could get his head caught in the handles. It's my guess Annie made a cushion of her sweater, and Wanda left it so that her aunt would see it and be touched by her kindness."

Again Bud gave me the two-eyebrow treatment. I plunged ahead anyway. "But Gerry, unlike Wanda, dislikes cats. In fact, he's afraid of them. So it's natural he'd open the French doors while he was here in hopes that at least Arthur would go out and leave him alone. He brought the bag because it contained a replica of The Black Hawthorne from the Smithsonian gift shop. He took the real vase, then smashed the replica and put liver on the mantel so Paddy would climb up and get blamed for the broken ginger jar. He figured his aunt would never know he'd taken the real one. If you move quickly," I suggested, "you can probably catch him at Dulles Airport. He'll have to go through Customs, after all."

I allowed myself to preen a little when Bud called an hour later to say that Gerry Simpson had been arrested. I may have allowed references to Jessica Fletcher to pass my lips when Bud reported that Gerry had declared a black hawthorne ginger jar as a souvenir.

I lost my complacency when Dr. Adzakian, chairman of the Chinese Art department at the Smithsonian and unofficial advisor to the D.C. police department, declared the ginger jar a fake.

The only thing that made up for my chagrin was what Bud described as the very real dismay on the face of Gerry Simpson.

"He really thought we were putting him on," Bud said, tucking into the leftover goulash I'd microwaved for him. "He thought he had the real thing, I'm sure of that."

"Which means," I began slowly, wary of making another blunder, "that somebody substituted ginger jars before Gerry made his move."

"I still think the old lady did it herself," Bud said. This was a theory he'd propounded more than once during my three weeks of cat-sitting. "I know if I had a valuable ginger jar and a houseful of cats, I wouldn't just leave the thing on the mantel."

"But you aren't Mrs. Simpson-Phelps," I argued. "She loves her cats and she loves her vase and she doesn't see any problem with—"

"Okay, so what happened, Sherlock?" Bud challenged.

"Wanda."

"When and how?" This was said through a mouthful of goulash.

I remembered the wine-colored doctor's bag. What reason could she have had for carrying it from her car into her aunt's house—except as a convenient receptacle for The Black Hawthorne?

Bud woke up a District of Columbia judge, got a search warrant signed, and had the ginger jar—the real one, this time, according to Dr. Adzakian—before Mrs. Simpson-Phelps's plane landed the next day. Since Wanda was in custody, I drove to Dulles Airport to meet my neighbor's plane.

After she'd heard everything, she leaned back in the bucket seat of my little red Honda and said, "Thank goodness you were there, Nikki. I can't thank you enough for what you've done for me. I don't know how I can ever show my gratitude."

"Oh, there's no need—" I began, but Mrs. Simpson-Phelps cut me off with a sudden cry of inspiration.

"I know," she said triumphantly, "I shall change my will and leave YOU The Black Hawthorne!" She turned to me, her face radiant, "And the cats, too, of course."

Carolyn Wheat:

Carolyn Wheat spent 20 years as a Brooklyn defense attorney, a useful background for such courtroom mysteries as *Mean Streak* and *Dead Man's Thoughts*, both published by Berkley Prime Crime and nominated for the Edgar Award. Her short stories include Agatha winner, "Accidents Will Happen" and "Guilty as Charged" which won both the Macavity and Anthony Awards. Carolyn lives and writes in San Diego, and is also a respected teacher and mentor for other writers. The Wild Bunch in this story are her own much-beloved pets, two of whom ended their lives in the Old Cats' Home. She is currently a defelined cat lady.

NO FREE VACATION

by Kathleen Keyes

"Five minutes to Paradise," I announced to my friend Holly, as she stuck her face out the window of my old VW bus. Veering west, the ocean came into view. The sunlight danced on the waves like diamonds.

"I can't believe that hairy-armed P.I. you work for is letting us stay here—rent free!" Holly said.

"Aw, Jasper's okay, Hol," I said as I turned on Tide Street. "Here it is," I sang as we pulled into the driveway.

"Yahoo," Holly exclaimed, reaching for the shoes she had tossed aside hours ago.

A heavyset woman, whose bright red hair clashed with her bright pink muu-muu, met us as we pulled in. She waved as if we were long-lost friends. In the other hand she held a bright green plate stacked high with big, chocolatey squares. Jasper had warned us about his neighbor, Mona McHenry. "She has a heart as big as the body it's set in," he said, "but she'll talk you into a coma if you let her sit down."

He was right. We were barely out of the car before she started a lengthy monologue about her recent trip down south, to visit her sister. She continued talking as we unloaded the car and made our way to the front door.

Trying to think of excuses for not inviting her in, I threw myself between the front door and the determined drone. She continued talking and walking, backing me into the house.

"Oh, my word," wailed Mrs. McHenry, pushing her way past me. "Someone has been here." Her face was screwed into a look of puzzlement.

"Pew!" said Holly, holding her nose. "Whoever was here didn't empty the trash."

The smell was like incense and old socks, and there were two wine glasses and an ashtray on the coffee table. I put down my suitcase and stood in the middle of the living room, surveying the little house and its contents. Holly started to pick up the ashtray.

"Wait, Holly," I said, raising my hand in traffic-cop fashion. "Don't touch anything. Mrs. McHenry, go back to your house and call the police."

"Why . . ." she started, then gave out a tiny, squelched scream, dropping the plate of brownies.

Holly rushed over, then stopped with a gasp. An open door at the end of a short hallway revealed a bedroom. Inside, a bedside lamp lay on the floor. A twisted, blood-stained sheet hung over the side of the bed. The three of us, glued together, tall, slender Holly, round, redheaded Mrs. M., and short muscular me, edged our way down the hall. No one was there.

"I'll call," Holly whispered. A nanosecond flashed by before the words registered.

"No!" I yelped, frightening poor Mrs. McHenry. "No," I said again, in a calmer tone. "We don't want to get finger prints on anything." I may only be Harry Jasper's Girl Friday, but I do know that much about crime scenes.

"I'm on my way," said Mrs. McHenry, and dashed out the front door.

* * *

"Welp, looks like someone decided to do a little entertaining in an empty beach house," said Lt. Morehouse of the San Morez Sheriff's Department.

"Entertaining?" My brain slammed against the casual indifference of this simple deduction.

"Welp, ya' got two wine glasses, a messed-up bed, no witnesses and no body."

"How do you know there aren't any witnesses?" I forced out. "You haven't talked to anyone!"

He scratched his chubby chin. "Welp, Mrs. McHenry, here, lives right next door. She'd probably notice if someone was gettin' murdered." He chuckled. He was the only one to find humor in this statement.

"Mrs. McHenry was gone for a week," I said. "Maybe this happened while she was gone. And what about the blood on the sheet!"

"Like I said," drawled the lieutenant, "looks like someone's been watching the place and, when it looked good, decided to have a little free vacation. Maybe had a little rough sex . . . oh, sorry, Mrs. McHenry," he added, looking like a little boy caught saying a bad word.

By the time Lt. Morehouse and his band of bumbling crime-fighters left, it was getting dark. Declining Mrs. McHenry's invitation to stay at her house, Holly and I left to find a motel and something to eat.

Neither proved difficult, since tourists are the livelihood of California coastal towns. Perhaps tomorrow I'll even be able to taste the food, I thought, as I finally laid my weary head on the smoky-smelling pillow at the Sleepy Harbor Motel.

After a restless night, I peeked out through the curtains to a sunny, clear morning. Holly was still snoozing as I pulled on my jeans, sweatshirt and tennis shoes, but woke when I opened the door.

"Did I over-sleep?" she mumbled.

"No, Hol. It's early. I'm going for a walk on the beach."

"You want me to go with you?" She yawned out the words as she rolled over to face the wall.

"No." I chuckled. "I'll get some coffee on the way back." I really wanted to walk alone. I needed to clear the cobwebs out of my brain and decide what to do next.

One thing for sure, I didn't want to waste my two-week vacation thinking about the ineptitude of the San Morez Sheriff's Department!

A brisk walk on the beach—just what my tired body needed. The air was crisp and smelled of salt water and fresh kelp. The damp sand was studded with broken shells and tiny pieces of colored glass, tossed and ground by the ocean into smooth, opaque pebbles.

"Nope, not leaving yet," I said out loud.

I stopped at the motel office to get coffee. A woman was sitting behind the counter and didn't look up when I walked in. Lucy Avery, Manager, said a small, copper-colored placard on the counter.

"It's fresh," she said, still looking down. "Heard there was a problem at Jasper's place last night."

"News travels fast." I contemplated Holly's tastes. Regular or Almond Mocha Java?

"Uh-huh. Guess you'll be checking out," she said, reaching for the registration book.

"Yeah," I said, then added, "We'll be staying at Jasper's."

Now she looked up, eyes wide. I picked up the cups of steaming coffee and backed out the door. I didn't look back, but I'm sure she watched me all the way to my room.

"What?" Holly squeaked, looking like she'd swallowed a gnat. "Are you nuts? We can't stay at Jasper's place. It might not be safe!"

"Of course it is, Hol," I said, trying to sound nonchalant. "Whoever was there is gone. Probably left when Mrs. McHenry got home. Besides," I fluttered my eyelashes, "Lt. Morehouse will protect us."

Holly clutched her throat and fell on the bed. "God, now I know we'll be murdered in our sleep."

An hour and a stack of pancakes later, we pulled back into the driveway on Tide Street. Mrs. McHenry darted out of her front door, smiling and waving wildly.

"That woman must have radar," I muttered.

"Nothing could get past her," Holly replied.

"You're back!" Mrs. McHenry cooed. "Come have some coffee. I just made a Peach Berry Crumb Cake!"

By this time, she had Holly in tow and was reaching for me. Out of the corner of my eye, I caught a glimpse of someone at the back of Jasper's house. He was running toward the public beach walk.

I bolted away, nearly knocking Mrs. McHenry down. I sprinted to the top of the stairs that led to the public beach. A couple with their children, building castles in the sand, and two women walking along the edge of the water were all I could see.

Coming back, I noticed Jasper's sliding glass door was open. I entered the house cautiously, trying not to touch the sides of the door. Scanning the room, I crossed to the hall. Aware that I had stopped breathing, I closed my eyes and forced a deep breath. The slider squealed behind me. I spun around to see Holly and Mrs. McHenry leaning in the opening, hands on door and frame to keep themselves from falling in.

"Don't you two ever watch *Columbo* or *Law and Order*?" I cried. "There may have been fingerprints on that doorway!"

They jerked back, but too late. I continued through the house. Satisfied it was unoccupied, I stepped back outside. There was the culprit, in Mrs. McHenry's back yard!

"Outta my way!" I yelled.

The trespasser heard me and dashed for the beach. Luckily, he was rather heavy for his chosen profession, so I was able to catch up with him. I flung myself on his back. We both tumbled to the ground. I hoped I'd knocked the wind out of him, as I had no idea how I could subdue a man twice my size and half my age!

Mrs. McHenry lumbered across the lawn, Holly close behind. Mrs. M. plopped down on the culprit's legs. "He won't get away now!" she said, victoriously. He'll never walk again, I thought.

"Get off! Get off!" hollered our suffering prey.

"Mike?" Mona McHenry's eyes popped open like she had heard a voice from the other side. Puffing and groaning, she got to her feet.

"Michael Shawn McHenry!" she admonished, tapping her foot near the temple of the panting, perspiring fellow under me. "What the hell are you doing here? You're supposed to be in school in San Diego."

"I got kicked out," he said, burying his forehead in the grass.

Mrs. M.'s kitchen looked just like her. Lemon yellow walls, flouncy polyester sheers with little embroidered butterflies on the windows and an old, oversized O'Keefe and Merit stove. We sat around a wooden table, painted robin's egg blue, drank sweet tea out of oversized, brightly colored mugs and waited for the stream of chastisement to subside.

We learned that Mona's redheaded boy had been living in the darkness of Jasper's beach house. He'd planned to stay there until he had the nerve to tell his mother he'd been expelled from school.

I asked if he knew anything about the blood on the sheets. He said he had invited a girlfriend up for a few days while his mother was gone. The girlfriend was still in bed when he walked downtown to get donuts Thursday morning. When he returned, she was gone and everything was the way we found it.

Mrs. McHenry had come home from her sister's that afternoon. Holly and I arrived on Friday. Mike had been staying with a friend, ". . . trying to figure out what to do," he said.

"Why didn't you call the police?" we chimed in unison.

He said he'd thought about that but was afraid of being arrested for trespassing. Or worse—suspected of hurting his girlfriend!

"Why did you come back today?" I asked.

"I wanted to be sure I hadn't left anything behind," he said, looking into his cup.

I waited until Mona was busy at the sink, winked at Holly, and motioned to Mike to come outside with me. Once there, I asked him what he couldn't say in front of his mother.

It seems he had been dealing a little Marijuana to support himself until his roommate in San Diego could forward his monthly stipend from his mother. He had gone back to the house to get his stash, which he'd hidden in one of the Chinese wicker boxes stacked in the bedroom. After the glare he got for admitting he had been in bed with his girlfriend, I wondered if his mother would be any more upset about him using or selling pot.

"Oh, great," I said. "Yesterday we didn't have any idea who, what or how. Now we have a possible victim and a whole list of possible suspects."

"Well, not exactly a list of suspects," Mike said. "Gary Booker was the only one buying from me."

"Who's Gary Booker?" I asked, pulling Mike down the driveway by the arm. I could see Mona's back at the kitchen door and knew Holly had run out of things to keep her occupied inside.

"Our mailman," he replied. "He's the one who suggested I stay at Jasper's place."

The mailman—the one person who always knows when someone is away. And when they'll return. I wondered if Mike's was a special case, or if Mr. Booker was the unofficial, underground vacation rental coordinator.

Soon Mike, Holly and I sat in Lt. Morehouse's office.

"Hmm," he said, rubbing his stubble. "Still no body. Still no murder. Lucky for you, Mike McHenry. You'd be the prime suspect!"

"You still don't think there's been a crime?" I said in amazement. "What about the fingerprints? And the blood? And where's Mike's girlfriend?"

"Whoa. I never said there wasn't a crime. I said, without a body we can't say there's been a murder." He poured himself another cup of coffee. "The blood is being tested . . . and I suspect the red hairs we found are from young McHenry's head and the long brown ones from his girlfriend's." Mike looked pale.

We'd gotten all the information we were going to from Lt. Morehouse, so we went back to the beach house. Mike followed us in. Guess he didn't want to face his mother yet.

"I just don't understand why someone would want to hurt your girlfriend," I said. "Was she involved with someone else? An ex-boyfriend maybe? A drug problem of her own?"

He assured me she had no ex-boyfriend problems and, aside from an occasional glass of wine, didn't drink or even smoke pot.

"Well, if it wasn't a deliberate plan to get her, then there must be something else the intruder was looking for. Something valuable—at least to him. Whoever it was must have thought the place was empty. She just surprised him . . . or them."

What could be important enough to kill for? I wondered if Jasper had something to do with it. Some files or evidence on a current case, maybe.

"We'll search the property," I announced. I considered calling Lt. Morehouse, but decided against it.

"What are we looking for?" asked Holly, as we pulled linens out of cabinets, clothes out of closets, and turned drawers upside down.

"Anything unusual," I said. "Anything hidden, taped-up, or disguised as something else."

"And when you find it, you can give it to me," said a voice from the hall. A man carrying a gun appeared in the doorway. "And thanks for doing the work for me."

"Damn," Mike muttered.

"I guess you know this guy," I said in his direction.

"Booker," he replied.

The mailman. "So, Mr. Booker, what have you got hidden here? Did you kill the girl?" I asked, more boldly than I should have.

"What girl?" he sneered.

"The bimbo you were sleeping with, you moron," said a voice behind him.

He pivoted, forgetting his hostages. Mike threw his arms around him, knocking the gun out of his hand. It slid down the hall.

"That's the lady from the motel," squeaked Holly. A small copper placard with "Lucy Avery, Manager" on it, flashed in my mind.

Lucy, Gary Booker and Mike McHenry dove for the gun, landing in a heap in the narrow hallway. I joined the dog-pile, working my way under the pile. I grabbed the gun and slid it toward the bedroom. "Get it, Hol!" I shouted.

"I'll take that," said another voice, not from the tangle on the floor.

"Lt. Morehouse!" I sure was glad to see him. "What are you doing here?"

"Mrs. M. saw you come in. When she noticed Booker, here, standin' outside watchin', she gave me a call."

"Told you nothing could get past her," said Holly, grinning.

"So, what's going on here?"

"I think Mr. Booker has something hidden he doesn't want anyone to find," I volunteered. "He must have thought the house was empty Thursday morning. When Mike's girlfriend surprised him, he shot her."

"Mike's girlfriend?" stuttered Lucy. Then, looking at Booker, "You mean she wasn't . . ." Lucy crumpled to the couch. "Oh, God."

Just then, Mona McHenry bounded in the back door. "Good news, Michael! Your friend Valerie called. She said some crazy lady ran in the house last Thursday, calling her a bimbo and waving a gun. Valerie tried to get up but the lady shot her. Just nicked her, but she bled like a stuck pig. As soon as the woman left, Valerie grabbed her stuff and didn't stop until she was back in San Diego."

"It was you, wasn't it, Lucy?" I asked.

"Yes," Lucy confessed. "I thought Gary was having another one of his affairs." She looked at Mike. "I thought I'd killed her."

"Guess my boys missed a bullet hole behind the bed last night," mused Lt. Morehouse.

Holly rolled her eyes. I had to bite my lip.

Lt. Morehouse took both Lucy and Gary out in handcuffs. Mike and Mona went home. The house would be crawling with police in the morning, but the lieutenant agreed to let us stay, with a promise we wouldn't do any searching on our own.

Holly and I collapsed on the couch.

The telephone rang. "Hey Kiddo. This is Jasper. Just thought I'd call and see if you found everything okay at the beach house."

Kathleen Keyes:

Kathleen Keyes is a native Californian and twenty-five year resident of the Central Coast. Now retired, after seventeen years working in a state mental hospital for the criminally insane, she has rediscovered the pleasure of creative reading and writing. She is a member of Sisters in Crime, national and local, and Central Coast Mystery Writers. Her stories have been published in SLO Death, More SLO Death and Nefarious e-zine.

What's a cop to do when his only witness to murder is a swan with an attitude?

SWAN SONG
By J.A. Lucas

Like a teenaged groupie following Fresno mayor Allen "Bubba" (In The Heat Of The Night) Autry, I returned to the scene of the crime early in the morning, yawning from the late hours I'd already put in there the night before. For the past two days the Central Valley weather was having its way with us. The promiscuous tease had seduced the country into thoughts of a long, easy autumn, then followed with a contemptuous slap of bitter cold. I shivered; too bad it wasn't spring. I could see where this acre and a half of park would be a blooming eye-opener.

My boss, Chief Detective Inspector Thomas, had already staked out the area. The man must never need sleep. Beside which, he'd been born a cross between a terrier and a bloodhound. Nothing escaped him, and working as his partner this past year beat all the courses I'd taken at the Academy. Thing was, he didn't talk much except when flim-flamming a suspect. On the job he grunted, twitched those graying eyebrows, or pulled on his ear lobe and pursed his mouth. Words, when they came, were pithy and direct.

Thomas was hunkered down on the muddy slope near the large pond to get a different perspective of the crime scene. In his warm brown jacket and slacks he looked like the Duncan Water Gardens' resident toad. I was hard put not to laugh.

Better cool it, Brian-my-boy, I told myself, it's way too early in the case to make with the wisecracks. I watched him closely. By interpreting the body language I could follow his thinking: Last night at early dusk the deceased, sixty-seven-year-old James Mercer, sat here on the bench where he could enjoy the shenanigans of water fowl and kaleido-scopic clusters of koi.

Not many people visit the gardens when it's cold, and James Mercer probably counted himself the park's only plea-sure seeker. The caretaker stated that he always made rounds before he closed the gates at seven. He'd greeted Mercer yesterday around five-thirty, then went to his greenhouse to nurse the Australian ferns. Between five-thirty and seven when the caretaker discovered the body, James Mercer had met with one or more people. The damp ground showed prints where he stood up and turned to face his assailant. The as-sailant stayed on the gravel path from where he stabbed a long, thin-bladed knife into Mercer's chest cavity. There was so much blood, the knife probably nicked his heart. Mercer didn't collapse on the spot, but staggered backwards, lost his footing, and slid down the muddy slope to the pond's edge. This scenario came from reading the evidence at the point of conflict. Around the body area was a great deal of disturbance. The assailant or an accomplice had tried to reach the dead man from a nearby footbridge and either jumped or fell into the pond. We had some good casts of footprints and a couple of hand impressions where he leveraged himself out of the water. Hand and shoe size profiled probable male. The unknown subject lifted Mercer's wallet and left trails of muddy water on the front of the dead man's coat. But he didn't touch the Rolex watch or two valuable rings that were in plain sight. Too scared? Too stupid? Both?

Inspector Thomas inclined his head my way. "Garbage companies?"

"Called 'em first thing," I replied. "Only one of those places was due for pick up. Company agreed to delay until tomorrow."

He gave a quick nod.

"What do you think of the partner for doing Mercer?" I asked.

Thomas tugged his ear lobe. Translation: Didn't feel right.

I agreed; Mercer's business partner, Arthur Bowden, would benefit from full ownership of the RV franchise, but he was a sharp one. Wouldn't have left the jewelry if he were trying to make this look like a robbery gone wrong.

I told Thomas I checked on Bowden's movements; nothing conclusive. He might have been able to drive over from his office to do the deed, but he would have had to fly back to fit in the time window of the crime and his secretary's statement—unless she was in cahoots or bed with her boss.

The dead man's wife was out of it. Frail Rose Mercer had recently been moved by ambulance to a hospice to finish out her days.

The couple had no living children or issue, only a niece by marriage on the wife's side. Said niece was the one Mercer planned on meeting today. She had left a message on his answering machine last night saying she and her husband had arrived and were staying at Motel Six. A deputy was dispatched to escort them here this morning.

Meanwhile, I watched the comedy routine of a white swan near the crime scene. Charlie Tooms, evidence technician, finished taking pictures of the site by natural light and turned his camera toward the bird. The swan immediately stopped its wing-flapping, backpedaling antics on the water and slid into serene behavior. I heard Charlie mutter, "Damn ham," as he snapped off a couple of shots to placate the bird.

To keep warm Thomas and I tramped along the park's trails, scoping out the territory to get a fix on the probably route the murderer took. The feisty bird followed us via water, making several bids for attention. I called him Harpo, as I surmised the comedian was a Royal Mute swan. Must have felt a real kinship with my boss.

At ten o'clock Deputy Horner escorted a couple through the front gate. Thomas and I waited in a gazebo built out over the pond. I studied the newcomers as they approached. Both were in their late thirties or early forties. Woman tricked out in well-worn coat and shoes and carried an out of shape shoulder bag. Arms crossed close over her chest, no expression allowed on her face except for a tight mouth. Was she grieving or missing her morning coffee?

The man was built big and running to paunch; orange gimme cap, flannel shirt, jeans. No coat and regretting it. Smiled a lot and looked clumsy.

A discreet cough and an eyebrow twitch from Thomas sent me back to check out the man's shoes. Damn, how'd I miss that one? They were white and shiny and new. Shirt and jeans appeared new, too. I called Thomas's brow and raised him a smirk.

Willy and Patty Stone were just up for a visit from Bakersfield. They had arrived after eight last night and left the message for Patty's uncle. Patty Stone insisted on doing all the talking now, while Willy stood behind her with a genial expression. I eyed the size of his hands and feet and checked off two more items that put him as a possible.

Harpo paced in the water.

When asked, Patty said they'd never been to the gardens before and had only been to Fresno once in the last seventeen years. Inspector Thomas became his most charming and took Patty Stone's arm to assist her up the path that led over the falls. Deputy Horner accompanied them.

I'd been given my instructions by brow signal and set about to become good ol' Willy Stone's new best friend. We walked along the pond's edge for a while before I let out a groan and motioned him to the nearest bench. Seated, I made a good show of a man with sore feet and slipped off my shoe.

"Oh, man," I said. "You know what they say about a cop's feet is true. What I wouldn't give to find a decent pair of shoes and not pay a month's salary for 'em." I turned to Willy. "Say, those look good; they comfortable?"

"Yeah, got to say they feel pretty good and din't cost no arm and leg." He stuck his feet out for me to admire his shoes.

"That so?" I asked. "But, I don't like spending a lot of time breaking in new shoes. How'd they feel the first day you wore 'em?"

"This is the first day, and they're just fine. Wife picked them up for me last night at that Target store just up the street from our motel. Only paid twenty-nine ninety-five for 'em."

"Can't beat that."

I motioned to another deputy as we stood up, and the three of us made our way around the pond opposite Thomas and Mrs. Stone. Ol' Willy and I got along like a house afire, and Harpo looked disgusted. Willy told me how he liked to tinker with motors and engines. Picked them up at swap meets, hokeyed them around until they ran again, and then sold them at the next meet.

"Well, hey!" I said. "You'll want to see how they got this baby to pump those falls. Come on over here."

I led the three of us along the path and over one of the foot bridges. I stopped at the bridge's end, bent down, and pointed for Willy to look at the area underneath. Willy started to squat to see, but jumped up immediately when he realized Harpo was making a dead set at him.

"Oh no, you don't, bird! You're not getting me again." He turned to me. "You know what that damned duck did to me yesterday? He goosed me, that's what he did. Never saw the like. You'd better be careful of where you set."

I stood up, "Yesterday, huh? That's mighty interesting. Did you fall into the water, maybe got all muddy too, and had to buy new clothes last night?"

"That's right. Couldn't get no jacket, though. But, I tell you that's the darndest bird—"

"Willy!"

Patty Stone hurried down the terraced steps and joined us. Thomas and Deputy Horner followed.

"Hi, Patty, I was just telling—"

"Willy, I told you I'd do the talking." Patty gave his arm a jerk. She turned to us. "Willy sometimes gets things confused."

"But, Patty, din't you see what that loco bird done? It was just like last night. You said yourself it weren't my fault. That bird has it in for me, I swear!"

A woman scorned has nothing on a scornful woman. Patty Stone called her husband several names all meaning fool and shoved him backwards into the water. Harpo swam circles around his prey and hissed.

We got Patty restrained and Willy out of the water and into some blankets. Charlie, the technician, signaled he'd gotten it all on film. With the testimony of the two deputies and evidence of the shoes and clothes we were sure to find, either in their car, room, or motel's garbage Dumpster, we pretty much had a lock on this case. Maybe we'd find the knife there, too.

While we waited for the warrants to be faxed to the patrol car, I looked fondly at the beautiful bird. If he'd been a dog, I'd have given him a bone. As it was, Harpo swanned his arrogance before an appreciative audience.

"Bravo, Harpo," I told him.

He acknowledged this as his due and glided off with a last twitch of his tail feathers.

Shivering and beat, Willy got tired of his wife calling him a fool and told us how Patty Stone had talked with her uncle earlier yesterday. Mercer told her of his plans to be here and said he would meet with them later at his house. Patty wasn't doing later and killed Mercer here with a kitchen knife she'd brought from home. She made Willy go after the wallet, and that was when he got his mud bath.

Patty figured that if Mercer died before his wife, she would inherit all from her aunt. But like a lot of greedy bullies, Patty Stone lacked the nerve to do the deed all by herself. So, she was done in by a smart bird and her own bird-brained husband.

Inspector Thomas and I made a farewell tour of the gardens. Back at the gazebo we watched Harpo frolic with a black swan.

"You know," I said, "I'm thinking of calling him Nemesis and writing a story about this case. What do you think of Nibbled by Nemesis as a title?"

Thomas pursed his lips and whistled silently. I waited him out. He rocked back on his heels with his hands in his pockets and smiled. "Two Stones With One Bird."

JoAnne Lucas:

JoAnne Lucas has won several awards for her short mysteries and most of them have been published. She lives, loves, & laughs in and writes about Fresno, California because someone has to.

BELLING THE CAT

by Maxine O'Callaghan

Melanie Veleaux began an asthmatic wheezing as soon as she walked into my office. Sinking into a chair, she dug in her oversized canvas bag for her medication, inhaled a long dose from the blue L-shaped tube, and sat, holding her breath for a minute.

I waited without comment, taking a moment to observe her and to wonder if peasant necklines, nipped-in waists, and full skirts had come back in style when I wasn't looking. I sincerely hoped not. The fashion suited Melanie, however. She looked like she belonged on a veranda down in Georgia, holding a parasol. Early thirties, I thought, but knew I might be off by as much as ten years. Long blonde hair curled around a delicate heart-shaped face. She had big smoky-blue eyes and the kind of petal-soft skin that meant she'd spent her life smearing on sun screen and moisturizers.

When she exhaled, I said, "You okay?"

She nodded. "It was your stairs. And so much stress. Besides, I usually don't go out this time of year because of the acacia."

"You mean the yellow stuff that's in bloom?"

"Yes. I'm very allergic to it."

"But not to cats?"

"How did you—?" She touched her dangling earrings—cute little enameled kitty faces.

"And I think that's cat hair on your purse," I said.

Okay, I admit it. I'm not above showing off.

"I am a little sensitive to Miss Bee Bee," Melanie said, "even though I've had shots. Still, I can't be without her. I adore cats."

Just thinking about the fuzzy little furballs relaxed some of the tension in her face. Not a bad thing because I did not want a medical emergency on my hands.

The respite didn't last long, however. She took another shaky breath and said, "I think somebody tried to kill me last week, Ms. West."

"Delilah," I said. "Tell me what happened."

"An attack—only much worse than this one. I always have an inhaler in my purse, but it wasn't there, and I nearly died."

"You think somebody deliberately removed it?"

She nodded. "I'm compulsive about checking for my medication, Delilah. I've learned to be. So I know it was there that morning."

"Who has a reason to want to kill you, Melanie?"

"Until this happened I would have sworn nobody did. But now—" she broke off, her eyes shining with tears.

"You suspect some one."

"Two people," she said miserably. "My husband and my best friend."

As a private detective I'm a skillful liar. Subterfuge is my life. So I'd readily agreed to come to Melanie's house a week later for Sunday afternoon tea, pretend I was working with Melanie on some charity function, and meet her two prime suspects. As a matter of fact, I'd jumped at the chance, since I'd spent the intervening time digging for dirt on Kenneth Veleaux and Jennifer Lowry and finding them both so squeaky clean they could have posed for a detergent commercial.

They both may have had opportunity, but motive? As far as I could tell, Jennifer had nothing to gain by killing her friend; Kenneth stood to inherit a substantial amount of money if Melanie died, but he already had a substantial fortune, enough so it appeared he taught history at the University of California, Irvine, because he enjoyed it and not for the salary.

Melanie met me at the door in another Southern belle cotton print dress. A fluffy gray cat wound around her ankles, studying me with eyes nearly as blue as her owner's.

"I feel so terrible about my suspicions," Melanie said, looking even more tense and haunted. "You have to find out if I could be right."

She led me into a room with overstuffed chintz-covered furniture, tasseled lamps, and baskets of silk flowers. French doors opened on to a patio where I could see what had to be wisteria climbing over a lattice-work trellis. Since I'd been following them around most of the week, I had no trouble recognizing the two people who greeted me with warm smiles.

Kenneth was a lean, homely man, but one who looked as comfortable in his own skin as he was in the tan chino slacks, blue cotton knit turtleneck, and well-polished loafers. Sturdy and trim in jeans and a pullover sweater, Jennifer exuded health and an easy-going good nature.

After introductions, Melanie said, "Sit, Mel, visit with Delilah," and hurried off to bring in dainty little crustless sandwiches, petit fours, and tall glasses of tea garnished with sprigs of mint—iced, even though it was a cold, rainy February day.

While we ate, the cat, Miss Bee Bee, played with a toy mouse until Melanie took a tissue from her purse and accidentally dropped a lipstick. The cat pounced on the silver metal tube and batted it with the skill of a hockey player skimming the puck across the ice.

"Miss Bonnie, you scamp," Jennifer said with a laugh and grabbed the lipstick away.

Despite Melanie's obvious strain and the fact that I was a stranger, Kenneth and Jennifer managed a graceful, lively conversation. My job was to observe, and what I saw was a solicitous friend and a husband who was constantly brushing Melanie's arm or her hand, that touch telling me more than all the dossiers I could put together.

Finally, Jennifer said she had plans for dinner and gave Melanie a goodbye hug. Kenneth excused himself, saying he had papers to grade.

When we were alone, Melanie looked at me with dread pinching her face. "Do you know who tried to—who took my inhaler?"

"Let me ask you something first," I said. "Your cat, Miss Bee Bee, Jennifer called her Bonnie."

"Miss Bonnie Blue," Melanie said. "Like Scarlett and Rhett's daughter."

I was afraid of that.

"My mother named me for one of the characters in Gone With the Wind," Melanie said. "I guess it's no wonder I just adore the book and the movie. But I don't understand what that has to do with anything. Do you know who hid my inhaler or not?"

"Yeah, I know."

I began to lift up the skirted edges of the chairs, finding the blue, L-shaped tube on the second try. "Remember when you dropped your lipstick?" I fished out the inhaler and tossed it on the floor where the cat immediately pounced and began to bat the thing around, right under the chair again.

"Bonnie Blue Butler," Melanie cried. "She did it!"

Thank God she said it, not me.

Maxine O'Callaghan:

Maxine O'Callaghan's 13 novels of mystery and dark suspense include a series that features Orange County, California P.I. Delilah West. Her short story, "Wolf Winter," was nominated for both the Anthony in the mystery field and the Bram Stoker Award for horror. Her last novel, *Down for the Count*, was nominated in 1998 for the Shamus Award for Best Private Eye Novel of the Year. In 1999 O'Callaghan received The Eye, Lifetime Achievement Award, from Private Eye Writers of America for her contribution to the field. O'Callaghan is a member of Mystery Writers of America, Private Eye Writers of America, Sisters in Crime, and the American Crime Writers League. A complete collection of her short fiction titled *Deal With the Devil and Other Stories* was published by Five Star in April 2001.

A LITTLE LIGHT ON THE SUBJECT

By Martha C. Lawrence

Being a psychic investigator has its pluses and minuses. On the upside, you occasionally get the opportunity to throw new light on a dark crime. On the downside, you have to endure the inevitable teasing from the cops. At the moment, I was getting an earful from Detective Callister.

"I thought you psychics didn't like to hear too much about the case ahead of time," he was saying. "Thought maybe the facts interfered with the vibes or something." He widened his eyes and made a rippling motion with his hand. I put a mental caption under the scene: Skeptical Cop Panto-mimes Aura Emanations.

"Guess I'm one of those psychics with a penchant for facts. It would really help me if you'd lay out what you think's important here." Most days are sunny in San Diego, and this Wednesday afternoon was no exception. Callister and I were traveling over a winding road that snaked through the scrubby backcountry northeast of the city limits.

"The first thing to know is that this is a kid-glove case," Callister said. "We're talking high profile. Don Shaw owned a big chunk of this town at one time, so a murder at the Shaws' isn't just any old residential homicide. These people are different."

"Different how?"

"Eight-thousand-square-foot house at the top of the hill. A Beemer, a Mercedes SL, last year's Acura Legend and a brand-new Cherokee in the driveway. Nobody's working nine to five, and there are four adults living there. Well, three since the body was found." He shook his head. "Rich people.

I'm telling you, they're different than you and me."

"Yeah. They have more money."

Callister took his eyes off the road just long enough to glare at me. "That supposed to be a joke?"

"A very old one," I said. "Sorry. Go on with the facts."

"Okay, facts. A nine-one-one call comes in last night. A girl with a fancy foreign accent, Christine somebody, says she's just gotten home and found Natalie Shaw in the back-yard. Between the hysteria and the accent it's hard to under-stand her, but we get that she's pretty sure Natalie Shaw is dead. We drive up there, find a twenty-two-caliber pistol in the bushes and a corresponding hole in the back of Ms. Shaw's head."

"So the victim was dead when you got there?"

"For at least a day. A stiff in the true sense of the word. And while we were dusting for prints and trying to make sense out of this Christine woman, the other two housemates came home."

"Kaye Shaw and . . . Alex Arno, right?"

"Yeah. Victim's sister and fiance'."

The traffic light at the intersection up ahead changed from green to red and Callister stomped on the brake. That was the first moment I saw. How do I describe such mo-ments? It's as if time comes to a sudden stop and I'm the only living thing, sole witness to a frozen world. These mo-ments speak to me: Pay attention, Elizabeth. Something's important here. But pay attention to what, I wondered now. Traffic lights?

Then the moment was over, and everything returned to normal. "No prints on the gun," Callister was saying, "and everyone had enough alibis to keep us digging for weeks."

"What alibis?"

"The medical examiner narrowed down the time of death to sometime late Monday afternoon or early evening. The boyfriend claims he was driving to L.A. at the time. No wit-nesses. The sister, Kaye Shaw, claims she was at the barn with her horses. No witnesses. The foreign girl who called in, Christine, claims she was on her way to a class at the university. When we asked her if her classmates could cor-roborate this story, she said that after she got there, she found out the class had been canceled. Likely story, right? But we tracked down the professor this morning, and it turns out she's telling the truth."

"Okay, so everybody's got an alibi. How about physical evidence?"

"Nothing. Like I said, no prints on the gun. At first we thought we had a robbery-homicide, since the victim was missing a pricey engagement ring, but nothing else was taken. The murder weapon was a family heirloom kept under lock and key in an upstairs cabinet. We're pretty sure this was an inside job."

"So you have three likely suspects. Sounds like this is a case you could easily handle without my help."

Callister tilted his head and looked at me as if I'd said something sensible for the very first time.

"No doubt. But like I said, this is very high profile. Lieutenant Gresham wants to close the case pronto. Like today. We're short on manpower right now, and he seems to think we'll save a lot of time by bringing you in. Says you can quickly point us in the right direction."

I smiled. This was the third case the lieutenant had thrown my way. I was a little concerned that he was expecting instant results, though. Ten years as a research guinea pig at Stanford had proved to me that while my psi ability is undeniably real, I can't turn it on and off at will. Which is why I have a private investigator's license. With most cases I devote as many hours to methodically poking around as I do to chasing down psychic flashes.

"Who am I to argue with the boss, right?" Callister said. "But I still can't believe I'm going out on a call with a psychic investigator." He shook his head. "Does the department actually pay you for this?"

"Yep. I may be different, but I'm not that different. I work for my wages just like you do."

                              * * *

The next three miles we rode in silence as Callister's car climbed the sage-covered foothills surrounding the San Pasqual Valley. At the crest of the range he turned onto a private drive. The luxury cars must have been tucked away in the six-car garage, because the circular driveway was empty when we pulled in and parked. I stuffed the case file into my all-purpose tote and walked with Callister toward the sprawling two-story hacienda.

"You exaggerated," I said as we neared the front door. "This house can't be an inch bigger than six thousand square feet."

We stopped under the towering entryway, and Callister pushed a lighted button on the wall. The grand scale of the place was intimidating. I half expected the Wizard of Oz to poke his head out and demand to know who was ringing that bell.

When the door opened, I saw that my wizard theory had been way off. Alex Arno was a thinking woman's version of tall, dark and handsome. Six two or three, he wore understated clothes that nonetheless announced a great body. His light-green eyes were as striking for their intelligence as for their unusual color. Right now they stared steadily at Callister.

"Hello again." His voice, deep and soft, put his sex appeal over the top. "You brought a friend, I see."

Callister glanced sideways at me. "This is Dr. Elizabeth Chase. She's working with the department on the case."

Alex's eyes met mine, and one of his eyebrows went up a notch. "Special investigator," I said. As if that explained anything. He stepped back and opened the door wider. "Please, come in."

Once inside, I went about my usual routine. I always begin with a walk-through, checking for psychic impressions. Visual images, gut feelings. My rational mind argued that the ritual would take hours in a house this size, but I pressed on, trusting that my feet would take me where I needed to go.

My initial instinct was to go to the back of the house. It may have been simple curiosity, since this was where the body had been found. I stood at a sliding glass door, looking out at a swimming pool surrounded by a wide brick terrace. Beyond the terrace the valley opened up in a magnificent three-dimensional backdrop. While I had the vague sense that something was significant about this spot, I saw no inner images, felt no gut feelings. As I say, I can't turn my psychic ability on and off like a faucet.

In time something pulled me back inside and up the stairs.

I felt drawn toward an open door at the end of the hallway. I popped my head inside and found Alex Arno. I wasn't surprised. It didn't take psychic powers to realize a lot of women must be drawn to him.

Alex was kneeling on the floor, disassembling an entertainment system. Around him were several boxes, some taped shut, others half full. Most of the shelves on the bookcase along the wall were empty.

"Go ahead. Ask me anything. I'm operating on about two hours' sleep, so I can't promise I'll be coherent. But I'll try." His attention was fixed on the back of an amplifier, where he was twisting a long, slender screwdriver.

"What do you do for a living?" I asked.

He looked puzzled. "Seriously? You really don't know?"

"No. Should I?" Perhaps Callister had told him I was a psychic and he was expecting omniscience on my part.

"I'm an actor." He pulled a wallet from his back pocket, flipped it open and handed it up to me. Inside was a laminated card from the Screen Actors Guild. "I play Jason on Malibu Shores."

Maybe it wasn't exactly a nine-to-five job, but a role on Malibu Shores certainly qualified as gainful employment. I recognized the name of the show but had never seen it.

"Sorry," I said. "I'm afraid I don't watch very much television."

He smiled. "That's okay. To tell you the truth, it's kind of refreshing not to be recognized." His smile disappeared, and suddenly my heart began to feel as heavy as if I'd just gotten news of a death in my family. I felt shock and depression. These weren't my own emotions. They were Alex's, coming into my body loud and clear. I examined the feelings for remorse, guilt—anything that would point to Alex's part in the murder. I found nothing but grief. Painful.

I handed his wallet back. "So you were engaged to the victim."

He put the billfold back in his pocket and stared at the carpet, nodding slowly. In the silence that followed, I watched his face and reminded myself that Alex Arno was an actor. Was the tear forming at the corner of his eye induced by some Method technique? I doubted it but couldn't be sure.

I broke the silence with the obvious question. "Do you

have any idea who might have killed Natalie?"

When he looked up, his features were tight and anguished. "I have a perfectly excellent idea who killed her. Kaye did. I assumed you people were here to arrest her. You are going to arrest her, aren't you?" He searched my face and, when he didn't find an answer, pressed his eyes shut. "Please don't tell me she's getting away with this. That cocky little—"

"Why would Kaye kill her sister?"

He picked up the screwdriver and resumed twisting. "She hated her younger sister. The kind of hate you see only in families, know what I mean? Like psychotic sibling rivalry. Anything Nattie got, Kaye wanted for herself. Attention, money, even me. I always knew Kaye had a thing for me. She finally came on to me a few days ago. I turned her down. Maybe she flipped over that. Who the hell knows."

"You've mentioned your thoughts about Kaye to the police?" He coiled some electrical wiring and tossed it into a box. "Of course I have. But they probably think I had a better reason to kill Nat than Kaye did."

"And what reason would that be?"

"Isn't the boyfriend or the husband always the first suspect?" I shrugged.

His shoulders sagged. "Natalie and I were having problems. We'd had a big fight." He gestured across the room with a sweep of his arm. "Hence the moving boxes. I have a place in North Hollywood, but off-season I lived here, with Natalie."

"Did she break off the engagement?"

"No. At least, she was wearing her engagement ring the last time I saw her."

"What was your fight about?"

He shook his head. "There's not a simple answer to that. Basically, Nat wasn't ready to make the compromises marriage requires. She was used to being independent. Traveled around the world alone." His smile returned. "Talk about a stubborn redhead. The engagement ring's a perfect example. She wouldn't let me give her a diamond. She had to get the ring on her own. She said it had to be a special stone."

Alex reached into his back pocket and retrieved the wallet. This time he flipped to a photo and handed it to me. I studied the picture. Alex and his former fiancee stood in a classic engagement-photo stance. Framed by a full head of shining red hair, Natalie's face was interesting but by no means classically beautiful. She was smiling warmly, her left hand resting on Alex's shoulder. My eye was immediately drawn to the gem on her ring finger, extraordinary for its size as well as its ruby-red color.

"Did that bother you, Natalie's independence?"

"No, what bothered me was not being together enough. I wanted her to marry me and move to Los Angeles. I was sick of this house meaning more to her than I did."

"This was her house, then?"

"Hers and Kaye's. Inherited from their father. Their mom died several years ago. Their dad left them the house and a portfolio worth God knows how much."

"All Kaye's now?"

"Until you arrest her."

"I won't be arresting anybody. I'm just a special investigator."

I wandered from Alex's room out into the hallway. As I neared the stairs, a door opened and a woman with pale-blond hair stepped into my path. She looked directly at me, and her dark blue eyes widened. She was young, nowhere near thirty yet.

"I'm with the police," I said. "You're the one who found the body?" She nodded and gripped the banister.

"Are you all right? You look as if you don't feel well."

"I feel horrible. I've never lost anyone this close to me before." Her European accent was quite heavy. Although she spoke excellent English, understanding the words required active listening.

"Were you related to Natalie Shaw?" I asked.

"No, although she was like a sister to me. We'd been very close since we met in Denmark three years ago. She was setting up a business in Copenhagen. That's what Nat did. She helped American companies get established in Europe: Madrid, Paris, Oslo, even Moscow. I worked for the company she set up in Copenhagen. I'd always dreamed of studying in the U.S. We talked about it a lot. Last year she offered to let me live here while I earned my college degree."

"So you've lost a friend."

"More than a friend. I'll probably return to Denmark now. Kaye doesn't like me, and I can't afford to stay on my own."

We stood in silence for a few moments, looking down at the first floor below. I opened myself to Christine's energy. This time I picked up physical sensations: a rapid heartbeat and rapid, shallow breathing. Fear. Brought on by the shock of discovering her friend's body? Or was Christine afraid because she had something to hide?

I turned to face her. "What do you think happened to Natalie?" "I don't know." Her blue eyes locked onto mine. "I'm trying to accept that either Alex or Kaye shot her, but I can't believe it." She looked down the hallway toward Alex's room and lowered her voice. "Maybe Alex did shoot her. The day before yesterday, they had a terrible fight."

"Alex and Natalie, you mean."

She nodded. "I'd heard them fight before, but not like that afternoon on the terrace. I was watching from that window." She pointed to the other end of the hallway, where a bay window looked out onto the backyard.

"Could you hear what they were saying?"

She shook her head. "Not really. Just their loud voices." But something registered in Christine's mind. I saw the memory flicker in her eyes.

"What was that?" I asked.

"What?"

"That thought," I said. "The one that crossed your mind just now."

She looked surprised but answered willingly. "I was just thinking that I did hear the last thing Alex yelled as Natalie walked away. He said, 'The hell with her!'"

"Do you know who he was talking about?"

Again she shook her head, more slowly this time. "No. After that I saw Nat get in her car and drive off. Alex went back inside, and then I heard him drive away, just before I had to leave for school."

"When did you find the body?"

"Not until a whole day later, yesterday around sunset. I went out to do a few laps in the pool and—" She put her fingers to her mouth. Her voice turned to a whimper. "I saw her leg first, under the azalea bushes. I knew it must be Nat. I recognized the shoe she wore. But her skin was gray . . ."

"What did you do then?"

She cleared her throat and steadied her voice. "I ran into the house and called nine-one-one."

"Were Alex and Kaye home?"

"I hadn't seen Alex since the day before, when he'd been fighting with Nat. He came back just after the police and the ambulance got here last night."

"How about Kaye? Was she at work?"

"No, Kaye doesn't have a job. She came home about fifteen minutes after Alex did. She'd been at the stable all day. She often is, with her horses."

"Was Kaye home the afternoon Alex and Natalie had the fight?"

"No. She didn't get home until after I had left for school."

"So it's possible that Kaye could have killed Natalie while you were at school."

"I don't know." Christine shook her head. "I just don't know."

Detective Callister appeared in the downstairs hallway and called up to us. "Could the two of you come down here a minute?" When we reached the bottom of the stairs, Callister led us into the living room. He glanced at Christine and pointed to the coffee table. "Do you want to explain what these were doing in your room?"

Christine and I walked over for a closer look. On the tabletop were a blue topaz necklace and a pair of pearl drop earrings. Callister stared hard at Christine.

"Kaye Shaw says she found them in your dresser drawer this morning. Says they belonged to her sister."

Christine looked up, dazed. "They did belong to Nat. She lent them to me. Kaye doesn't think I stole them, does she?" Callister didn't answer. "You don't think—" She looked to me, then back to Callister. "Am I in trouble?"

Again he didn't answer her. He simply walked out of the room. Christine and I watched him go. I hadn't liked the look on his face, and again I felt Christine's fear. I had the sense of a frightened animal, injured and unable to fend for itself.

"You might want to get a lawyer," I said.

"What? Is that policeman saying he thinks I killed Natalie over a pair of pearl earrings? That's ridiculous. Everyone knows how much I loved her. Besides, if I was going to kill and rob her, don't you think I would take something of real value, like her engagement ring?"

A similar thought had crossed my mind. I knew a little about jewelry, and the baubles on the coffee table weren't worth pilfering, let alone killing for.

A phone rang in the next room, and Christine excused herself to answer it. I took a seat on the sofa and pulled the case file from my tote bag. I turned again to a list of the evidence that had been gathered from the crime scene last night and reviewed the personal effects found on the victim's body: two diamond-stud earrings and a gold-plated hair clip. No engagement ring.

That was the second moment I saw. The evidence list was printed on a pale green police department form. As if I'd been staring too long, the paper turned a translucent, glowing red. Most people would chalk that experience up to eye strain. I knew better.

I walked through the kitchen area to the sliding doors at the back of the house. Through the glass I could see Detective Callister talking with Kaye Shaw on the terrace. She was unusually petite. Prettier than Natalie was in Alex's engagement photo, but somehow not nearly as attractive. She was listening to Callister with her slender arms crossed over her chest. She nodded, and Callister started back toward the house. I slid the door open for him.

"If you're going to interview her, I'd like to listen in," he said.

I closed the door behind him. "I'd rather you didn't." I made a rippling motion with my hand and gave him a self-deprecating smile. "Interferes with the vibes, you know?"

He rolled his eyes. "Whatever," he said and left the room.

For the next few moments I watched Kaye, standing at the edge of the terrace. She remained motionless, staring out across the valley. I slid the door open and walked out to join her. Kaye's close-cropped hair was a fiery, chemical-induced red. Her features in profile were stern.

"I'm sorry about your sister," I said as I approached.

"Thank you." She didn't turn to look at me when she

said it.

"I'm with the police," I said.

"I figured."

The air was temperate, but at that moment I wanted a jacket. I rubbed my arms to produce some friction. I didn't feel safe standing next to Kaye Shaw. I picked up a reckless, volatile energy that made me jittery, the way you might feel walking past a downed power line that could suddenly snake your way. I didn't know where to begin, so I started in the middle.

"I've been talking to your housemate, Christine. She thinks that perhaps Alex Arno killed Natalie."

Kaye was shaking her head before I'd even finished my sentence. "That's ludicrous." She thrust her hands into her jacket pockets. "I've already told the police that I'm certain Christine shot my sister."

Kaye was a terrible liar. Her eyes darted away from mine like cockroaches scuttling from the light.

"Why would Christine do a thing like that?" I asked.

"She lost her head in a jealous rage." Kaye directed her comment to the sky overhead.

"She was envious of Natalie's possessions, you mean? Her jewelry and whatnot?"

Kaye looked up at me through mascaraed lashes. "Christine is in love with Alex," she said. "She couldn't bear the thought of losing him to Natalie."

More likely Kaye couldn't bear the thought of losing Alex to Natalie, I thought. "Christine says Alex and your sister had a bad fight the day before her body was found. Isn't it possible that he could have shot her in anger?"

I could see Kaye's hands balling into fists inside her jacket pockets. "Alex? Never. But Christine was desperate. She knew she couldn't stay on here once Natalie got married."

"Have you asked Christine to leave?"

Kaye wrinkled her nose. "I assume the police will arrest her. She stole my sister's jewelry, you know."

"Is that right?" I tried but failed to catch her eye. "What about Alex? Will he be leaving too?"

Kaye's fingers worried the contents of her right-hand jacket pocket. "There's absolutely no reason for Alex to leave.

He'll always be welcome here."

The front Kaye put up was as brittle as icicles. I wondered if rattling her would break something loose. "If your sister had married Alex, they would have moved to Los Angeles. Isn't that right?"

"Possibly. I don't really know," she said coolly. Her fingers continued to fidget.

"Now Alex is leaving here anyway, isn't he?"

Kaye didn't answer. Her attention was fixed on a hawk circling over the valley.

Hard questioning wasn't getting me anywhere, so I tried flattery. "This is such a beautiful spot," I said.

"I grew up on this property," Kaye said dreamily. "I'll never leave it." Her jaw was set and the hint of a smile played on her lips.

"I suppose if Natalie had moved to Los Angeles, she would have wanted to sell the property and split the proceeds."

Kaye didn't speak. She merely crossed her arms over her chest again and shrugged. My eyes were drawn to her jacket pocket. That was the third moment I saw. The insight came as a vivid mental image of Alex and Natalie's engagement photo. The picture appeared in exacting detail, right down to the victim's ruby-colored engagement ring.

Years of experience had taught me to trust these unbidden visions, and I thrust my hand into Kaye's jacket pocket. She turned to defend herself, but too late. My fingers found the hard metal and brought the ring into the light. The stone glittered in the rays of the setting sun. My confidence was replaced by bafflement. To my utter disbelief, the gem was a clear, bright green.

Kaye looked at me with disdain. "Do you always go around picking people's pockets?"

I handed the emerald back to her. "I'm sorry. I thought . ."

I expected her to throw a fit and demand that I leave the premises at once. Instead, her enigmatic smile reappeared, and she turned back toward the view.

Why wasn't she angry with me? Her reaction was odd, as if she were trying to protect our mutual dignity by pretending the scuffle never had happened.

She pointed toward the east. "That's the San Diego Wild

Animal Park over there," she said in the same dreamy voice. "Sometimes at night the wind carries the sound of the lions' roaring all the way up here from across the valley."

Clearly something wasn't right with Kaye Shaw. Last night paramedics had dragged her sister's corpse out from under the azalea bushes, and now she was waxing poetic about lions. I played along.

"Isn't it strange the way the big cats are so lethargic in the daytime? It's as if they change into entirely different animals in the darkness." In the next few moments I thought about what I'd just said, and about how the changing light affects all living things: plants, animals, human beings. That was the final instance I saw, only this time it came as a flash of understanding. About change, about light.

"Kaye," I said casually, "would you come inside with me for a moment?" She turned to me slowly.

"Why?"

"I'd just like to finish talking inside. It's so beautiful out here it's distracting me." I smiled. "Humor me. I'll only take a moment or two more of your time, I promise."

"Well, I'd rather . . . Here, let's sit on the bench over here. That way you can turn away from the view if you want to."

"I really need to go inside." I took her by the arm and gently guided her toward the house. "Please, this won't take but a minute."

She followed along complacently enough at first, but the closer we got to the house, the more she resisted. As we neared the back door I could hear her heels scraping across the bricks.

"You have no right to be handling me this way!" she snapped. But tiny Kaye was no match for me, and pulling her into the house was almost too easy. I flipped the light switch on the wall and led her into the center of the kitchen. Again I reached into her pocket and brought out the ring. Under the glow of the incandescent lights the stone that had been bright green in the sunlight glowed red as a live coal.

"Alex was right," I said. "You are cocky, holding your sister's engagement ring right under our noses."

Her perfectly painted mouth formed a little O. But she recovered quickly and started talking fast. "Natalie's engagement ring was a ruby. Everyone thought so. You're making a mistake. This clearly isn't Natalie's ruby."

"Everyone thought so?"

She tried to snatch the ring from me. "I'm telling you that's not Natalie's ruby!"

I held the ring high above her reach and studied it through squinted eyes. "No, it's her alexandrite," I said. "Catherine the Great's favorite gemstone, named for the czar Alexander of Russia. Natalie bought it to honor her own Alex, didn't she? Alexandrite looks red indoors and in photographs, under artificial light. But out in the sunshine it turns green. Only the finest stones make such a complete color change. This is an exceptional specimen. Natalie probably found it on one of her business trips to Moscow."

"It doesn't prove I killed her."

"The last time anyone saw this ring, Natalie was wearing it, and she was alive. How did a dead woman's ring get into your possession?"

Kaye's eyes were no longer darting away. They bored into mine, radiating hate and determination. "It doesn't prove I killed her," she repeated.

Someone coughed. I looked up to see Detective Callister in the doorway. Kaye whirled around at the sound.

"I think we had better discuss this at the police station, Ms. Shaw." Callister stepped forward and took Kaye by the arm. "Let's go." As he led her away, Callister caught my eye, made a rippling motion with his free hand, and winked.

Martha C. Lawrence:

Martha C. Lawrence is the author of the popular mystery series featuring psychic detective Elizabeth Chase. *Murder in Scorpio* won her nominations for the Edgar, Agatha, and Anthony awards in 1996, and was followed by the critically acclaimed sequels *The Cold Heart of Capricorn, Aquarius Descending*, and *Pisces Rising. The Ashes of Aries* will be published in the fall of 2001. Inspired by her own real life psychic experiences, Martha's novels have been published around the world. Web site:
www.marthalawrence.com

BUILDING
OF
CHARACTERS

by K. M. Kavanagh

I was running out of time. The deadline was three weeks away, and I hadn't even started an outline. My course note-book had each progressive lesson completed and filed into its respective divider, but it lacked one thing—the story for my final grade.

Last fall, I enrolled in Mystery I at Cuesta College. That's where I met Derek. We discussed characters, and when Derek stated he'd found many of his at Maggie's Diner, the local off-campus coffee house, I didn't believe him.

After two cups of Maxwell House, he'd convinced me. A few more dates there, and I realized I'd fallen for Derek's one-dimpled smile. Red-checkered tablecloths, antique lamps that didn't match, and dark wood paneling carved with gen-erations of graffiti became my second home and our special rendezvous place.

Writing romance stories had always been easy for me. Too easy. As a mystery writer, I'd envisioned pages full of suspense but instead, my page was full of half-finished para-graphs with big red x's crossed through them.

I glanced at Derek; dark curly head bent over a legal pad, concentrating on his next episode of Sergeant P. Flannigan. My lover sat with note cards spread around him like a wall, shutting me and the rest of the world out.

He grabbed a french fry, munching on it without look-ing up. Then sensing my distress, he asked, "News events?"

I snatched up the headlines I'd listed, cleared my throat and read: "'Lost child found at friend's home; gang-related shooting in Oceano; manhunt for an Arizona killer; and a private plane makes an emergency landing at Hearst Castle.' See, Derek, truth is stranger than fiction."

"Skip the news, Mel. Do the exercise."

Derek had ignored my last comment, refusing to get involved in an issue we never agreed upon. Sighing, I glanced two booths down at an older couple with a daughter who appeared to be in her late teens.

I scribbled: "Golden hair fell forward hiding most of her delicate features except for the long eyelashes lowered shyly. But tight jeans exuding teenage hormone overload belied her feigned innocence.

"Mother's enormous cornflower eyes avoided her family. With glasses perched on her nose and lips pursed together, she examined the calendar section of the Tribune.

"Father's greying hair receded slightly, and shadows underlined tired eyes. Glancing around, he sized up each contender for his daughter's affection."

Instinctively, Derek reached for the page. I waited for the criticism which I knew would follow. It didn't. Instead, his hazel eyes shone with approval. "Good description. Now, WHAT IF . . ."

". . . they're going to a movie and can't agree on one."

"That's an incident, not a story."

"It has conflict." Immediately, I realized my mistake and mentally prepared myself for what he'd hit me with next.

"What's the 'teetering point'?"

"The daughter refuses to see another heavy drama. Her father agrees."

"That pulls your story forward, but what character decision will change their lives from that moment on?"

"Lately, they've argued over trivial issues, but the outcome is always the same. The father sides with his daughter; the mother fumes in oppressive silence."

"Let's heighten the conflict." He scrawled something beneath my description.

"Derek, you have a warped mind!"

I'd spoken too loudly. I waited until the people at the table nearest us turned away, then whispered, "He doesn't look like a pervert."

"His wife looks tense."

"Only because she can't smoke in here, and she's dying

for a puff."

"How do you know?"

"I got a close look at her in the bathroom."

"And . . ."

"Elementary, my dear. Age lines around her mouth. Cigarette ash by the toilet. The nicotine cloud still lingering over the stall."

Derek laughed. "Okay, Sherlock, cross incest off your list. Try another angle."

"No, I need a fresh target."

"How about the couple in back?"

I nodded, then wrote a brief paragraph: "Outfitted in the latest biking attire, the 30-something couple studied their Thomas Guide. While loading up on complex carbohydrates, they calculated the mileage for their next trek."

Derek finished reading just as the tanned couple rose to leave. The man paid with plastic, then they walked briskly by our table.

Wasn't fair. They were a decade older than we were, but in far better shape. Caught up in our drama, we craned our necks over our neighbors to see which top-of-the-line mountain bikes the fit couple would hop onto. They climbed into a Beamer instead.

"Dammit, Derek, I need a story." I hated the whiny sound issuing forth from my mouth, but was too desperate to stop it.

Derek calmly ordered coffee and pie for us—Maggie's specialty—then returned to his story. I crumpled up my paper and loudly tore off a new sheet.

I couldn't help myself. I envied Derek. Brought up by a journalist father, writing came naturally to him. Several articles he'd written had been published in the Sun Bulletin. Though Derek denied it, he still remained the teacher's pet. Small wonder. He'd finished one mystery by midterm, and now he'd almost completed another.

Yet, despite Derek's success, he helped me. He quizzed me relentlessly on setting and tone, created thought-provoking exercises for characterization, and gave me hints on plotting and dialogue. His strategy had worked; I'd become a better writer. Now if only I could think of a story for my final grade.

Just then, Delores, our waitress, brought our order of steaming vanilla decaf and fresh pecan pie. Mmmmm! Maggie was famous for her pie; it was hard not to drool. I gave Delores a quick smile, then settled in to devour my dessert.

I'd barely swallowed a bite when someone new entered the diner. Pushing aside a stray lock of thinning hair, the stranger glanced around nervously. He wore jeans and a plaid shirt on a build as average as his height. Despite the mouse-brown hair that looked as if it hadn't been combed in hours, I pegged him as nondescript. But then as he walked past us, I realized I was dead wrong. Something about his eyes frightened me.

The stranger's eyes were ice-blue and as cold and emotionless as a reptile's. Except his seemed deadly, like those of a hissing snake right before it strikes. The man slipped into a booth in the shadowy corner. Though it was hours before sunset, that area didn't benefit from a window's sunny warmth. His presence seemed to chill it even more.

I shivered. As I warmed my cold fingers on my coffee mug, I tried to think of ideas that excluded the stranger. But I soon realized I couldn't stop formulating conjectures about him. Finally, I gave in to my obsession and sketched out a storyline.

"Milton B. Bottenheimer, a lonely introvert, married the first woman he bedded. His nagging mother harped at him constantly, bringing up this mistake and others he'd like to bury. Goaded into a mortgage he couldn't afford, Milton was pushed beyond his credit limit. Coming home early one night, he caught his wife in her lover's arms. Seeking sympathy from his mother and finding none, Milton was finally pushed beyond his personal limit. Three bullets fired from a Taurus semi-automatic put an end to his torment. Despite efforts to hide the bodies, the Arizona police found two. They began a statewide manhunt for him."

Before I could tone down the more melodramatic parts, Derek snatched the paper from me and read it. Between stuffing pie into his face, Derek burst into fits of laughter. I hoped he would choke.

"What's wrong with it?"

"Jeez, Mel, don't you think you got a little carried away?"

"It's an exercise in imagination," I said. Embarrassed, I grabbed my paper back and stuffed it into my notebook.

"Aw, honey, I didn't mean to make you mad." Derek moved to my side of the booth, trying to put his arm around me, but I shrugged it off.

"I'm not mad! Just stop making fun of me." Sirens sounded in the distance, but we waited in silence until the check came. I pulled out my wallet.

Derek pushed my wallet aside and said, "You can't afford this."

"Only because I didn't get a scholarship."

"C'mon, that isn't fair."

It wasn't fair. I was so ashamed I'd said that. I touched his arm lightly, then said, "Sorry. Maybe I'm jealous because I can't write like you."

"Jealous? Look, Mel, I've been writing for a long time. Anybody can follow a formula. But that's not your writing style; you must follow your heart."

"I never thought of it that way. Thanks." Then I kissed him. As he pulled me closer for a second and more substantial helping, the lady at the next table shrieked. Startled, we looked at her.

The elderly woman cowered behind her husband. Drawn by their terrified gaze, I looked toward the back corner. My mysterious stranger was pointing a gun at the chest of Delores, whose face was pale with shock. The man looked around nervously, suddenly aware of the patrons and how many eyes were on him.

"Everybody stay where you are," the stranger warned, "or my wife gets it!"

I knew the guy must be crazy because Delores is a widow. My heartbeat thudded in my ears. My throat dried in fear. Derek seemed to be suffering from adrenaline overload, muscles so wound up that I clutched my notebook for comfort.

We stood as perfectly still as possible and watched as the gunman maneuvered Delores toward the front entrance. Their progress was slow and methodical, and I became increasingly nervous with each step toward us and started shaking uncontrollably. Just as they reached our table, I accidentally dropped my notebook onto Derek's foot. In one fluid motion, he kicked the notebook and it flew into the gunman's shin, scattering papers everywhere.

Angry, the man turned, pointing his gun at Derek, as I threw hot decaf into his face. He shrieked in agony. Before the gunman could recover, Derek leaped forward, snapped the guy's wrist outward and shoved, sending gun and man flying backwards.

He landed on the nearest table, launching food and utensils in every direction, while its occupants scurried out of the way. Just as the man reached for his gun, Delores conked him with the sugar container. He crumpled to the floor while sugar spilled down over his inert body.

Delores smiled nervously, explaining in her Texas drawl, "Thought he might want sugar with his coffee."

The man was still out when the police units skidded into the parking lot, sirens wailing and lights flashing. Minutes later, the uniformed officers had the dazed perpetrator cuffed and in the back of a squad car. The officers checked on us shortly after checking on Delores. Then after offering a perfunctory thanks, they advised us not to interfere in future criminal matters.

I stared numbly at the aftermath of our adventure—remnants of spaghetti and meatloaf dinners splattered on a wall and nearby tables, shattered glasses, broken plates and notebook papers scattered in every direction, a table and chairs upended—then noticed the other casualties around me. Amid the chaos, an older couple clung together as if they'd never part, a man gently comforted both wife and daughter, and Delores smiled at the policeman who'd draped a blanket around her.

While we waited to make our statements, Derek bent over my papers and started to gather the less damaged ones for my notebook. All I could do was watch and say a prayer of thanks that he hadn't been hurt. When he finished his task, he handed my notebook back. He looked at me tenderly and said, "Don't worry, Mel. I'll help you fill in the missing pages."

"No, I don't need my notebook anymore. I think it served its purpose."

"No argument there," Derek said, flashing me one of his one-dimpled grins.

A short while later, we joined the cook, Delores, and the remaining patrons who'd gathered together to gawk at the drama playing out beyond the glass front entrance. Seemed as if every sheriff and police unit in SLO County wanted to get in on the action. They'd surrounded the parking lot and a brown Camry that needed rust remover. We watched in morbid fascination as the coroner removed a dead body from the Camry's trunk. Naturally, we were stunned that the corpse's face bore an uncanny resemblance to Delores.

I was the first to notice that the car sported an Arizona license plate. Of course, I pointed this out to Derek. Then I pulled him aside and in my best Sherlock imitation said, "You see, Watson, truth is stranger than fiction."

"No, you're stranger, and that's the truth."

I rolled my eyes, then glanced at him curiously. "By the way, how'd you do it?"

"Do what?" My love was showing me a side of him I'd never seen before. He shuffled his feet nervously while he avoided looking directly at me.

"You know what I mean. How did you kick my notebook into that creep's shin?"

Derek grinned sheepishly. "I never told you what I got my scholarship for."

"I thought it was for journalism."

"That's what everybody assumes," he stated nonchalantly, but his face blushed the bright red of the checkered tablecloths.

"Well, what did you get a scholarship for?"

"I should think it would be obvious, Holmes. Soccer, of course."

Karen (K.M.) Kavanagh

Karen (K.M.) Kavanagh dabbles in fantasy, mainstream and non-fiction writing, but mysteries are her first love. Though her stories have appeared in periodicals such as *Dogwood Tales* and *By-Line*, and have placed well in national contests, K.M. believes Sisters in Crime will help her to achieve her next goal: a published mystery novel!

METAPHOR
FOR MURDER

by Sue McGinty

I was seventeen the first time I visited Lorna. Seventeen and ripe for adventure. "Lorna" was an antebellum mansion transplanted, incongruously, to the hills east of Santa Barbara. In 1938, it rose high above the fog of California's coast, radio commentator Louis Labrador's memorial to his wife. Alas, poor Lorna—former Atlanta heiress, former child star, currently dead.

Mr. Labrador's estate house rivaled another further up the coast, one owned by a man so powerful some were afraid even to speak his name. Be that as it may. By the late '30s, Lorna had become the place to go for a wicked weekend party. The Hollywood elite might not like Louis Labrador's isolationist radio diatribes, but they loved his free food and wine.

So how did a seventeen-year-old kid wangle an invitation to Lorna? I had connections. You see, my grandfather was character actor Josef von Strasser. Grandpa came to unwind after his latest film. Or so he said. The real reason was to keep an eye on me. It was Friday night, and I was ready for anything—or so I thought.

"Canape', Miss?" A waiter held out a silver tray piled with shrimp.

"No, thank you, my man," I said, trying not to sound like what I was, a hick from the hills of Arizona.

While the first winter storm of the new year raged outside, I stood apart from the others in the gathering room, at the end of a long and very drafty central hall. I felt as Alice might if she'd tumbled into the film set of *Gone With the Wind* instead of a rabbit hole. The pink damask settee and chairs were dwarfed by high ceilings and wide windows, draped in lush velvet. The floor-to-ceiling bookcase stood next to a hearth big enough to roast an ox, and the piney smell of crackling logs filled the air. I shivered, allowing the fire's warmth to move across the bare back of my sequined dress.

A silver-foxed woman approached, waving an ivory cigarette holder in one hand and balancing a cocktail in the other. "Some shindig, eh?" she asked gaily. Without waiting for an answer, the woman swiveled, hips first, and moved toward more important prey.

Fingering the wave in my bobbed hair, I counted seventeen other perfectly coiffed heads. The men in tuxedos and tails, with pomaded hair, swaggered like penguins. Women in bright-and-bare satin gowns inspected each other for sagging necks and extra ounces. Several people gathered around the man playing Gershwin on a baby grand. Across the room, Grandpa huddled with three other men. A few guests, like me, warmed themselves in front of the fire.

A man in a white ten-gallon hat spoke earnestly to a woman whom Grandpa had pointed out as a hot new reporter for *Movie Fan* magazine. Her fellow journalist and chief rival, the veteran Amanda Pickle, lurked nearby, glaring at the couple. Amanda stood by a table, caressing a sword that looked like a Civil War relic. That is, until a man in a dark suit jogged over and whispered in her ear. The hand fell to her side and her eyes scanned the room guiltily.

"Cocktail, Miss?" Another waiter held out a tray laden with stemware.

"Uh . . ." I hesitated, saw Grandpa's back turned, and chose a Martini. "Thank you, my man."

I held up the glass. The drink matched my blue-white diamond ring exactly. The stone caught the firelight and my palm began to itch, as it always does when I see something exquisite. The diamond was so large, so . . . so. I would think about *that* on Monday.

To banish the unwelcome thought, I took a large gulp of the Martini. The raw alcohol burned my throat, bringing tears.

My dress, which fit like a sequined glove, had no pockets for a handkerchief. Through a haze of now-liquid mascara, I peered down the hall to see an older man lumber through the massive oak front door. He was dressed all in black and shaped exactly like an egg. Stopping in the entryway, he shook rain from his umbrella onto the marble floor. In a flash, the man who had whispered to Amanda Pickle jogged toward him. They conferred briefly, then the older man walked back out into the storm. I'd seen that egg-shaped man somewhere, and not long ago. But where?

Oh-oh. My grandfather approached, the drink waiter in tow. Grandpa made a clucking sound, removed the glass from my hand, set it on the waiter's tray, and waved him off.

"Come, Zelda. Allow me to introduce you to Beau Calhoun and Anna Gatesby," he said, referring to Hollywood's newest beautiful couple. "Anna and I are old friends," Grandpa said, in precise, measured tones, pointing to a mustachioed man and a blonde woman by the piano. With a no-nonsense grip, my grandfather took me by the elbow.

As we moved across the room, people stared at us, a tall gentleman of the old school and his petite young companion. Though his name wasn't a household word, Josef von Strasser had had small, but pivotal, roles in most major films of the '30s. Now with Hitler poised to sweep across Europe, my grandfather was worried. It might soon be hard for a German actor, even a skilled one, to find work.

"Beau, Anna," my grandfather said, approaching the couple. They tore their eyes from each other and looked around. "I would like you to meet Zelda, my granddaughter. She is visiting me from Tucson, Arizona."

"Tucson, you say? How quaint," Anna said.

"Yes," Grandpa said. "After we came here from the old country, my son moved to Arizona, while I remained on the coast."

"That was lucky," Anna said, dryly.

"Yes, Hollywood has been good to me." Grandpa ignored the barb. "I have even arranged a screen test for Zelda, on Monday morning," he added, with a smile of pride.

"What am I, invisible or something?" Beau reached over and took my hand into the two of his. "Hi ya, kid." His hands were warm and smelled of lemon. "I'll bet you have a contract by Monday afternoon." At that moment, I found out hearts really do stand still.

Anna removed my hand from Beau's and placed it in her own. She smiled warily. "So, your name's Zelda von Strasser?" I nodded. "I'm sure the studio moguls will change that moniker in a hurry. What with all the Nazis—" She stopped abruptly as Beau elbowed her in the ribs. Grandpa's eyes grew wide, but he said nothing.

At that moment, James, Mr. Labrador's new secretary, entered the gathering room. He had shown us to our rooms earlier. He adjusted round, tortoise shell specs, held up both hands, and waved for attention.

"Ladies and gentlemen," he said in clipped, British tones, "Mr. Labrador has just rung up from his broadcast studio in Los Angeles. He has been detained by the storm." James held up pale fingers for silence as the crowd groaned. "Please carry on, enjoy your dinner. If the storm abates, he'll join you for the cinema afterwards." He made a sweeping gesture toward a room down the hall. "Dinner is now served in the ballroom. I'll be 'round if you have questions."

"Zelda, please allow me." Beau held out his arm. I grabbed it without a second's hesitation. As the four of us glided down the hall, I felt a sudden chill. Once again, the egg-shaped man stood in the entryway. This time it was James, the secretary, who moved toward him.

I forgot about the egg-shaped man—Alice in Wonderland had now become Cinderella at the ball. My eyes popped at the sight of three enormous crystal chandeliers, which hung from a ceiling at least twelve feet high.

"Like those?" Beau asked.

"They're beautiful."

He whispered, "Fake. Like everything else around here." I tried not to fan the air. Beau's hands might smell like lemon, but his breath reeked of garlic.

A long, narrow table had been placed in the center of the room. Eighteen gold chairs flanked the table. On the rose damask tablecloth, a king's ransom in fine silver refracted the firelight from yet another enormous hearth. *Silver.* Surely that was real. My palm itched again. I glanced at Grandpa, who gave me a warning shake of his head.

Using place cards, we found our seats. Grandpa and I sat across from each other; Beau and Anna found themselves at the far end of the table, close to the fireplace, the "hot seat," according to Beau.

The first course arrived; raw oysters. They looked like, like . . . well, you don't want to know. I ignored the slimy things and turned to the man on my right. Without his ten-gallon hat, he was pretty cute, with fine blonde hair and blue eyes.

"Wolf Montana," he said in an "aw-shucks" accent, sticking out a large paw. He wore a silver and turquoise cuff-style bracelet.

"Pleased to meet you." I shook his hand, extending my fingers to graze the bracelet's dappled blue-green stones. My father was a jeweler back home in Tucson. Unless I missed my guess, Wolf's bracelet had been handcrafted by the Navajo.

"Wolf is Century Studio's new cowboy actor," Grandpa explained.

"Dora Golightly," said the blonde woman to my grandfather's left; the reporter talking to Wolf earlier. "May I have catsup, please?" she asked the waiter.

Amanda eyed the Heinz bottle and quickly set it in front of her rival. "There you go, darling, 57 varieties, just like you. Stuff yourself," she purred.

Grandpa ignored Amanda and turned to Dora. "I have heard nothing but good things about *Movie Fan's* new reporter." He took her hand in his and brought it to his lips, looking aside long enough to give me the briefest of winks. "My granddaughter Zelda."

"Charmed, I'm sure," Dora answered, shaking catsup over her oysters until they resembled a nosebleed.

"I hear tonight's after dinner movie is *Saratoga*," Wolf said. "Too bad about Miss Jean Harlow."

"Yes, it's interesting to see the scenes where they used a double," Dora said, between mouthfuls. "Throws the studio into a tizzy when a star dies in mid-picture. Why I remember when Lorna Labrador died . . ."

"I'll bet," I said, trying to nod wisely. I had nothing to contribute to this very "in" conversation. I picked at my oysters, so my silence wouldn't be so obvious.

When the main course arrived, Wolf lost interest in the Hollywood shoptalk. Instead, he applied himself to piling curried chicken, peas, and rice on the back of his fork, patting them into a tidy mound with his knife, and with a rolling motion, popping the fork, upside down, into his mouth. Grandpa ate that way too, and I always feared he'd stab himself in the tongue.

"Wolf, are you from my home state, Arizona?" I asked, as a way to make conversation. When he hesitated, I added, "New Mexico, perhaps?"

"Neither," he said, wiping his mouth with a pink napkin. "Real name's Smith and I'm from Butte."

"Butte?"

"Yup, the capital of Montana." Seeing my puzzled expression, he asked, "Get it? Montana, Wolf Montana."

I got it all right. What I didn't get was why a man from Montana wouldn't know the state capital was Helena. The nuns at Santa Clarita hadn't taught me much, but they had managed to pound the 48 state capitals into my thick skull. A movement under the table caught my eye. I looked down just in time to see Dora's pointed toe make solid contact with Wolf's cowboy boot.

Interesting. Century's new star property might not be who he claimed to be. Something was definitely rotten and it wasn't the oysters.

Or was it? Suddenly, Dora set her fork down and stared at the plate, her face green as the curry. One waiter whisked it away as another placed the desert—pie ala mode—in front of her. Cherry juice swirled into pale ice cream, like blood on snow. She rose unsteadily, resting red-lacquered fingertips on rose damask. "Sick. *So sick.* Excuse me." She fled the room, a hand over her mouth. With narrowed eyes, Amanda Pickle watched her departure.

* * *

In Mr. Labrador's personal theater, I scrunched down in my seat, checked my tiny, jeweled wristwatch. Almost eleven, time for the film. Amanda Pickle had said that Mr. Labrador usually screened his late wife's childhood movies for weekend guests. Tonight was an exception. *Saratoga* had created a sensation last year, largely because of the untimely death of its star, Jean Harlow. A strange choice for a grieving man, I thought. But then Mr. Labrador wasn't here.

"Sit here, Grandpa." I patted the seat beside me, gazing at the chintz covered, floral walls. Tacky, I decided.

"Thank you, Zelda my dear." He took my hand. "Did you enjoy your dinner?"

"It was okay."

"Well, are you having a good time?"

"Oh, sure." The truth was, I felt a strong sense of foreboding. Come on Zelda, I thought, don't be a goose. I put my other hand over my grandfather's and smiled into his gray eyes.

"Can we sit with you?" Beau and Anna appeared next to my grandfather.

"Of course, of course," Grandpa said, a bit too heartily. "But I reserve the right to sit next to my granddaughter." Was I wrong, or did he give Beau a "hands off" look?

While Beau and Anna settled in, I looked around. People clustered in small groups throughout the theater. Behind us, Amanda Pickle joined a couple of journalists in animated conversation. Wolf sat like a lone cowboy near the back. I hoped Dora was okay. Lights dimmed and we settled in to watch the film.

Soon after the short subjects began, a door opened at the back of the theater. I looked around to see a man backlit by the hall lamp. I couldn't make out his face, but there was no mistaking that build. The egg-shaped man took an aisle seat in the last row.

* * *

I blinked when the lights came back on, yawned, and stretched both arms over my head. My watch said 1:00 A.M.

"So Zelda, what did you think?" Beau asked. He scooted over next to me. Grandpa, whispering that he wasn't feeling well, had excused himself midway through the film.

I chewed my lip for a second. "It was okay, for a horse racing movie. I thought it was really obvious when they used a double for Jean."

"I agree," Anna said. "Too bad she couldn't have gone out on a high note."

"Yeah," Beau sighed. "I'm gonna miss that little filly." He looked sad for a moment, then slapped his knee. "Hey, how about we all take a midnight swim?"

"In this weather?" Even the thought gave me goose bumps.

Anna laughed. "The pool's indoors, silly, right under this theater."

I chewed my lip again. "Better not. I need to check on my grandfather."

"We understand, kid," Anna said, cuffing me on the arm. She turned to Beau. "Last one in gets to skinny dip."

Anna tore up the aisle, with Beau in hot pursuit. Upon reaching the last row, she stopped dead. Stopped dead and let out a shriek they probably heard in San Francisco. Beau rushed to her side, and the others followed. Without knowing how I got there, I found myself among them. The egg-shaped man still sat in his aisle seat, his black vest slashed across the chest. With unseeing eyes, he stared at the ceiling. To this day, I remember the blood.

"My God," a journalist exclaimed, "Someone's murdered Winston Churchill!"

* * *

Around 3:00 A.M., I fought relentless wind and rain on the walkway from the main house to Grandpa's room in the two-story guest house. Feeling more like Rapunzel than Cinderella or Alice in Wonderland, I'd spent a restless two hours in one of the loft bedrooms, listening to rain pummel the windows. Listening and thinking of what had happened. I remembered that I'd seen Winston Churchill's picture in *Life* magazine. He had warned of the danger Hitler presented to Europe and even the United States. But why was Winston Churchill in California, here at Lorna of all places?

Right now, I just wanted to go home. But that was impossible. The highway had washed out above Ventura and there was major flooding on the lower road leading to the mansion. Also, the telephones were dead.

We learned this when James appeared in the theater, just after Anna found the body. The main gate was locked, as were all the others. He ordered us to remain in our rooms, prisoners on this hillside. A major political figure had been killed. One of us was his murderer.

James hadn't mentioned guards, but they must be out there. Still, no one stopped me when I dressed in dark clothes, sneaked out of my room, crept downstairs, and let myself out the front door into the storm. I'd worry about getting back in, later. Right now, I had to see if Grandpa was all right.

I opened the door of the guest house and stepped inside the dimly lit foyer. Thank God, the lights still worked. The guest house seemed eerily quiet after the tumult outside. That's funny, I thought. Grandpa said his was the only room on this floor, but there were several closed doors here. At the far end, one stood ajar. Grandpa's, I hoped.

As I opened the door, a lightning bolt lit the room like a scene from hell. Something beckoned me into the room.

I glanced over my shoulder, and seeing no one, slipped in and shut the door. I found a lamp near the bed, switched it on. My eye went straight to Wolf's bracelet. So, this was his room. Why would he go off and leave his door ajar, especially with the bracelet in plain sight? To say nothing of a murderer on the loose. I slipped the bracelet over my wrist. Nice. Very nice. I scratched my palm; it itched fiercely.

Now I heard voices in the hall. Heart pounding, I froze. A man and a woman. Wolf and a woman. Wolf and Dora!

Frantically, I looked around. They mustn't find me here. Hide, Zelda, I thought. The closet? There didn't seem to be one. The bathroom? Too exposed. At the last possible moment before the door opened, I switched off the light and dove under the bed. The duvet was too short to provide much protection, but it would have to do. I lay on my stomach, arms splayed in front of me. That was when I noticed I was still wearing the bracelet.

"Strange. One of the servants must have closed the door," Dora said. "I can't believe you'd go off and leave it ajar. You mustn't be so careless, honey."

"You are too tense, my darling. Do not worry so much. These stupid Americans—" Wolf's "aw-shucks" accent had become briskly Teutonic.

Two pairs of feet appeared beside the bed, dripping puddles on the floor. "I'm freezing. Why did you insist we take that stupid walk?" Dora whined. "And I feel sick again."

"You needed the air, my dear. A person who covers good oysters with American catsup deserves to be ill."

"Very funny, Wolf."

Wolf laughed. "I thought Frau Pickle poisoned you."

At the word "Frau," my foot jerked back in surprise. An object close to the wall clattered on the bare floor.

"What was that?" Dora leaned over, lifting the duvet. I shrank back in terror.

"It is nothing. Relax, my darling." Wolf pulled her back up. Lightning again filled the room. I could see the bones in their feet, like those x-ray machines that showed your toes in new shoes.

Instinctively, I grabbed the object by my foot, felt it. Was it? No, it couldn't be. It was. The Civil War sword! This must be the murder weapon. I began to shiver uncontrollably.

"Oooh, I hate storms," Dora cried, as thunder rolled across the heavens. "Wolf, I know you have a flask of brandy. Please honey, give me just a little nip for my nerves." She slumped down on the bed. Wolf sat beside her and began rummaging around. Would he notice the bracelet was gone?

"Turn on the light, honey," Dora begged.

"No, I like the darkness. Here," Wolf said finally, "drink this."

"That's better." I heard swallowing noises, then, "Hold me, Wolf Baby, I'm so scared."

Bodies moved above me and the mattress began to jiggle. Oh no, I breathed. Not here, not with me under the bed. Thankfully, the mattress stopped and after a few seconds of silence, Dora sighed, "I feel better now. I'm going back to my room and try to catch forty winks."

"That's an excellent idea," Wolf said.

The door shut softly and Wolf settled back down. I'd have to stay put until he fell asleep. If he fell asleep.

In a few minutes, I heard loud snoring. Time to make my escape and tell someone—anyone—what I'd seen and heard. But what was my excuse for being under Wolf's bed? If I was accused of snooping—or worse—stealing a guest's bracelet, my movie career would be over before it began. And Grandpa would be so ashamed. Wait a minute, Zelda, I thought. We're talking about *murder* here.

I wiggled out from under the bed and paused, taking stock. My heart skipped a beat when the snoring ceased and Wolf began to thrash around. I wiggled back, kicking the sword again in my haste. Sugar! Now you've done it, I thought. But I got lucky, and the snoring swelled to a crescendo.

I was halfway to the door before I remembered. *The bracelet.* I crept back toward the bed and was just placing it near the lamp, when I heard, "What?"

Gasping, I whirled around. Another lightning bolt electrified the room. Wolf sat upright, staring at me. Staring, I soon realized, with sleepwalker eyes. He sighed mightily, sank back with a thud, and began to snore again. I tugged the door open and sprinted toward the foyer like Jesse Owens in the '36 Olympics. Straight into the arms of James.

* * *

"Baskerville, British Security," James announced to the guests hastily summoned to the gathering room, where we'd started the evening. Now everyone was dressed in nightclothes. Again, satin predominated, the men in black robes with long lapels, the women shivering in light peignoirs.

One of the journalists said, "Then you're not Mr. Labrador's new secretary?"

With a weary smile, James shook his head. "Unfortunately, no. This murder is a tragedy, not only for England, but for the United States as well. Mr. Churchill seems, that is, seemed, to be one of the few politicians, on either side of the Pond, who understands what Hitler is up to."

"But why was he here?" the man persisted.

James turned to me. "Miss von Strasser has a most extraordinary story to tell. I would like you to hear it from her."

I stepped forward and looked at the faces, all peering at me. James stood to one side, watching the guests intently. I took a deep breath. "I know who killed Winston Churchill."

Everyone in the room gasped. Well, I'd jumped off the dock. Now I'd have to swim.

I pointed at Wolf. "He did." They gasped again.

"That's flat ridiculous, little lady," Wolf said, putting a hand on his chest. "Why would I kill a British diplomat? I'm just a cowboy actor from Montana."

"No, you're not," I said. "You're a Nazi spy." Another collective gasp from the guests.

"Why do you think that, little lady?" Wolf was a better actor than a spy.

"Because you don't eat like an American, you eat like a

European, and you don't know the capital of Montana, for starters," I answered. "And one minute you talk like a cowboy and the next you sound like Hitler."

"That's mighty flimsy evidence, Miss *von Strasser*," Wolf said with heavy emphasis on the "von Strasser." He looked around the room, and several people nodded in agreement.

"I was under your bed and I heard you and Dora talking," I said. Now Dora's gasp could be heard above the others.

"What were you doing there?" Wolf asked warily, looking at Dora.

Dora answered for me. "I know what she was doing. I saw her eye your bracelet at dinner. She came to steal it."

A man literally materialized out of the woodwork, as one of the bookcases lining the wall swung back, revealing a secret door. Beyond it, I could see a circular stairway. Perhaps this led to Mr. Labrador's private quarters. Leaving the door open, the man handed James a towel-wrapped bundle. James unwrapped the bundle and cradled the Civil War sword in the towel, being careful not to touch it. On cue, the crowd gasped. The sword was covered with dried blood.

Wolf's eyes narrowed when he saw the sword. "It was you, von Strasser," he shouted at my grandfather, who sat across the room, pale and shaken. "You left the film early."

"And you're his accomplice!" Dora shrieked, staring at the sword and pointing a red talon at me. "I'd bet a dollar to a donut your fingerprints are on that." She rose from her chair and started for me, claws extended. I moved to one side, too close to Wolf, I soon realized.

"Just a minute, young lady," James said, grabbing Dora by the arm and leading her back to the chair.

"Wait. It could have been Amanda." Dora shouted, desperate now. "I saw her fondle the sword earlier."

"Be serious, darling," Amanda Pickle said. "Why would I kill Winston Churchill when you present such a tempting target?"

None of us saw it coming. Wolf jumped up, grabbing me and the sword in one fluid motion. Standing behind me, he put an arm around my neck, grasped the sword by the blade, and held it to the side of my throat. "One false move and the Fraulein dies," he shouted. Dragging me along on my heels, reluctant and terrified, he backed up toward the secret door, which was still open.

We were almost out of the room. Strange. The others seemed to be looking beyond me. I soon found out why. Wolf took one last step backward—straight into the arms of the egg-shaped man, who stepped out of the shadows beyond the secret doorway.

"What the hell?" Wolf spat.

With surprising agility, the man wrestled the sword away from Wolf and handed it to James. Wolf and Dora, who had run to his aid, sagged against the bookcase, the fight gone out of them. Several men in black rushed through the open door, surrounded the couple, and led them away.

"Second rate spies, definitely second rate," the man said, dusting his palms together. He looked around the gathering room at the open mouths, then bowed slightly. "Winston Churchill, the real Winston Churchill, at your service."

"But you're dead!" Anna Gatesby said.

Churchill leaned toward Anna, inviting her to pinch his chubby cheek. She did. He winced. "As you can see, I'm quite healthy. Unfortunately, the man who acts as my double on official missions has not been quite so lucky." He shook his head sadly. "Morse always did have a weakness for Anna Gatesby. Too bad it was his undoing."

"What are you doing here?" I asked, curiosity getting the better of good sense.

"That's official business and none of yours, young lady," James snapped.

Mr. Churchill waved his hand airily. "No, that's quite all right. I don't mind telling you, but it must go no farther. At the behest of His Majesty, I'm here to persuade Mr. Labrador to soften his isolationist position regarding the Nazis."

"And Mr. Labrador, unfortunately, is stranded in Los Angeles," James added.

Churchill nodded. "It's becoming more and more evident England is going to need American help if she's to resist Hitler. I'm asking you, as people of honor and good citizens, to let your knowledge of this night's affair stay in this room." He looked around, his eyes coming to rest on Amanda

Pickle. Amanda blinked.

"Okay, I'll admit Wolf had motive," Beau said, "but what about means and opportunity? Don't forget there were at least seventeen other people in that theater."

"Think about it," James said, smiling, "and you tell me what happened."

Beau fingered his mustache for a few seconds. "I've got it! At least I think so. Wolf sat in back, then picked his time and popped out into the hall. Several people came and went during the film, so it wasn't noticed. Dora waited close by with the sword she'd grabbed from the gathering room, after that hasty exit from dinner. Wolf slipped into the theater, stood at the back, and 'offed' the poor man during a loud part in the film. After all, it was a horse racing story. He just didn't figure on Churchill having a double."

"Like Jean Harlow in the film," I breathed.

"Exactly," James said. "I'm sure, when the road opens and the G-men arrive, Dora and Wolf will, as you Americans say, 'spill the beans.'"

"G-men are coming?" one of the journalists asked.

"The phones are dead."

"There's a short-wave radio here in the mansion," James said. "After all, this is a very isolated spot. And we had a tip. That's why Mr. Churchill brought his double. Too bad about Morse. Sorry to lose him. He was a good man, and he has a wife and young son at home."

"If you had a tip, why didn't you arrest Wolf and Dora right away?" Anna asked.

"A tip is just that, my dear; a tip. Besides, we were told the threat came from a German man and his American accomplice." He gestured towards Grandpa and me. "We suspected von Strasser here and his granddaughter. We thought that if we gave you two enough rope . . . but things got out of hand. Sorry 'bout that, old chap."

"These things happen," Grandpa said sadly.

"I saw the egg-shaped—I mean Mr. Churchill—I mean Mr. Morse—twice," I said, "once during cocktails and again as we were going in to dinner."

"Actually, you saw Morse once and me once," Churchill said. "We both love a good party, and we were anxious to join you, despite being told to stay out of sight until Mr.

Labrador arrived." He sighed. "Unfortunately, we didn't coordinate that awfully well, either."

"It doesn't matter," James said. He turned to me. "Zelda, I'm not going to ask why you were in Wolf's bedroom, because the fact that you were changed history." He looked toward Churchill, his eyes shining. "I can't imagine the consequences if this man had really been killed."

He faced the others. "My men and I will stay here and guard the prisoners until the G-men arrive. I suggest the rest of you call it a night." He consulted his pocket watch. "Or should I say, morning?"

In the half light, I walked Grandpa back to his guest house. His room was one floor below Wolf's. I'd gotten turned around in the storm.

* * *

It was a new day at Lorna, where nothing was what it seemed, where everything was illusion, imitation, a misplaced metaphor. The storm had spent itself and moved on. The Mansion road was open, telephones worked, and the highway would be repaired. Mr. Labrador would be here by lunch time. Too late. The party was over. Through the mist, we saw headlights from several cars coming up the hill.

"Probably G-men," I said.

"Undoubtedly," Grandpa answered.

"Grandpa, why were you and Dora both sick?"

He smiled. "It may actually have been the oysters."

"I'm glad I didn't eat them."

We walked a few more steps, then Grandpa stopped and turned to face me. "Zelda, our friend Dora was right about one thing. You were in Wolf's room to steal his bracelet." He sighed heavily. I looked aside, but he turned my face toward his. "Weren't you?"

"I just wanted to try it on," I said, my hackles rising.

Grandpa shook his head. "Granddaughter, you have a decision to make, one that will affect your entire life. You can be a film star or you can be a thief, but you cannot be both. Think about what you want."

I didn't have to think. I slipped the diamond off my finger, taking just a moment to caress its faceted surface. My palm no longer itched. "Will you return it for me, Grandpa?"

"Of course," my grandfather said, pocketing the diamond. He began to whistle, his breath making rings in the morning air.

Author's Note: This is work of fiction. There is no evidence that Sir Winston Churchill ever used a double for public appearances. He was named British Prime Minister in 1939, after the Munich Pact dissolved, when Hitler invaded Czechoslovakia and Poland.

Sue McGinty:

Sue McGinty loves to write historical mysteries for young adults. She learned the ways of teenagers raising three of her own. Her novel, *Shadows on the Rainbow,* takes place during World War II against the backdrop of the 1943 Detroit race riots. Sue's short fiction has been published in the anthology, *More SLO Death.* A former Detroit resident, she now lives in Los Osos, California.

DEADLY OBSESSIONS
A Zoe Morgan Mystery
by Kris Neri

I'd always joked that my obsessions would prove to be the death of me, but it was just a joke. After all, obsession isn't a dirty word in my line. I'm a professional triathlete— if I weren't driven to make it to the finish line before the other gal, I'd have to find a different way to pay the rent. Yet that didn't mean compulsive behavior had to take over my life as it had—I couldn't let anything go with less than my absolute best. But kill me? I never guessed how close my joke would come to being a reality. Nor how many other lives I would risk along with my own. I never dreamed how deadly obsessions could become.

* * *

When John Bricker called my sports agent to ask whether I'd stop by the hospital to see his son, I assumed he just wanted me to sign my latest Triathlon cover for a sick kid. It wasn't that unusual. While hardly a household name, I do have a following in fitness-crazed San Diego, where I live.

Even after I pushed through the door to Danny Bricker's private room, I still didn't associate the patient's name with the buzz on the triathlon community's grapevine. All I noticed at first was that someone had taken pains to introduce personal touches to the boy's hospital room—but that those items had been added with a level of precision that made Martha Stewart look like a slacker. The family photographs in sparkling silver frames were lined up in rigidly parallel lines on the nightstand, and the sheet folded down over the patient was so precise, it could have passed a marine inspection. Even the man seated in a shadowy corner sipped tea from an elegant bone china cup.

Then I focused on the broken boy beneath the neatly

folded sheet. At the tubes coming in and going out, at the pins and braces holding his shattered limbs together. The penny finally dropped. I remembered that Danny Bricker had been a seventeen-year-old triathlete on the rise—when a hit-and-run driver struck him during a training run along the docks in San Diego one cloudy night. Piling insult on injury, he'd been struck by an old van his family owned, which had been stolen the day before; the police found it abandoned a few miles away. Weeks later, the kid still hadn't emerged from the coma the accident put him in. They were classifying it as attempted murder.

My identification with this maimed athlete was immediate and vivid. Instinctively, I turned to leave. People think I'm so strong. It's true I have the grit to make my body keep going when most would cry out for mercy, but there are all kinds of strengths and all kinds of weaknesses. I just run faster than my fears. The idea of being immobilized like Danny Bricker was one of the worst of the fears that pursued me.

Before I reached the door, the man in the corner called out to me. "Ms. Morgan. Zoe, please." His voice caught before the admission he was about to make. "I need your help."

* * *

John Bricker persuaded me to stay. "Tea?" He gestured to a gold-trimmed teapot with a delicate lilac pattern and an empty cup and saucer, matches for his own teacup. "Or I can get you coffee if you like."

Coffee was too dehydrating for an athlete. "I'm a tea drinker, too." Only I guzzle mine from a mug I got free at the gas station. "That's a beautiful tea service."

He nodded. "The set was my wife's grandmother's. She treasures these pieces. I thought having family things around . . ." His voice trailed off in a wistful sigh.

I judged him to be in his early forties, though it was hard to be sure with the rigid tension controlling his face. His eyes were the color of steel and smudged below with the soot of fatigue. I locked my own eyes on him when he poured my tea, rather than let them drift back to the boy clinging to life on the bed.

After we sipped in silence, John said, "I hope you'll agree to find out who did this to my son."

I shook my head. "You've got the wrong girl. I'm an athlete, not a detective." Never mind that I acted like a detective when it suited me.

"You're what I need, Zoe. Someone who doesn't give up."

"What's there to pursue?" I asked. "I heard they charged the guy who did it. The paper said they found his fingerprints in your van."

He nodded. "Pepe Morales. He did some work around our house last month, and he used that van. There doesn't seem to be any doubt that our sometime handyman moonlights as a car thief. But did he leave his prints in my van when he worked for me, or when he stole it and hit my son?" John gave his wedding ring a nervous twist. "I have to know."

The anxiety I felt coming from him triggered a flash of inspiration. "You sound like you know who did it. Who...?"

"I don't *know* anything!" he snapped. "I'm—I'm . . . afraid it might have been Danny's mother, or his twin brother." His voice broke off. "Neither can explain where they were when it happened."

I looked at the ring he had been turning. "You're . . . divorced?"

His lips twisted ironically. "Happily married, I thought." He shrugged.

I felt sorry for him, but I still wasn't the one for the job. "You don't know what you're asking."

"I think I do. I saw your face before you turned to leave. I could see what being here did to you. But as strong as your need is to avoid what happened to Danny—that's how much I need to know. Can't you see that? I'm obsessed."

In the end, it was his appeal to our common homeland, Obsession, that made me agree to look into it. I didn't expect to learn anything the police hadn't. But I knew too well what it was like being haunted by the dark images that come in the night. Unfortunately, I also knew chasing away John's demons would just transfer them to me.

I went to see my friend Lou Pela at the SDPD. Lou's in homicide, not vehicular crimes. But he traded a marker for the chance to see the file, which he shared with me. Not that he did it happily.

Vexation flooded Lou's espresso eyes. "I don't know

why I keep helping you play cop, *chica*."

"Join the club. I can't figure out why I coach you for free, either." An amateur triathlete himself, Lou's race times had improved since he met me.

He grumbled quietly after that, while studying the file. "Open-and-shut, Zoe. The skid marks at the scene were Morales' signature."

"Car thieves have signatures?"

Lou nodded. "Some of them leave evidence of their driving pattern. The investigator on the case thinks the Bricker kid must have seen Morales with their van, and Morales had to silence him."

"What does Morales say? Does he admit to hitting Danny?" I asked.

"He cops to all the car thefts he's charged with—except for the Bricker van. He swears he didn't take it, and he didn't run down that boy." Lou frowned. "Why is Bricker fighting it? Most parents would want to lynch the guy."

I told him. Lou's ramrod spine slumped, and he ran a hand over his short-cropped hair. "Families, they just make you feel so warm inside." Lou flipped through the file until he found the investigating detective's impressions of the Brickers. "They are quite a bunch. Bricker was the only one who cooperated. His wife, Sharon, was hostile, argumentative. And the boy's twin, Eton—well, it seems there was some problem with his birth. Danny emerged the all-American boy, sleek and smart and strong. While Eton is—not. The kids at school call him 'Eat,' because he does it so much. Still, family tensions, don't make people killers."

Sometimes, they're exactly what does it.

* * *

I rode my bike over to the Bricker home, thinking how ironic it was that people kept coming to me to solve their problems. My life was just one finish line after another, each victory another deposit in the holes I kept hidden within me. People were just life's wallpaper to me.

Danny's tragedy hadn't lowered the family's standards, I saw when I reached the house. The lawn before the large home in the elegant Fleetridge section of San Diego was so green and even, it might have been painted on.

I'd been assuming all the precision I'd seen in Danny's

room had come from Sharon Bricker, even if the nurses told me she didn't spend much time with her son. I figured a woman with that tea pot and cups had high standards. But once she came to the door, I realized her attachment to the tea service must have been purely sentimental.

Sharon wore an unmatched pair of well-washed sweats, and her blond hair hadn't been combed today. It wasn't much after noon, but the smell that came off her told me her lunch had been the liquid kind.

Even though her husband had sent me there, I expected to encounter the same obstruction the police found, and Sharon didn't disappoint me. "The police are satisfied Pepe hit Danny. What right have you to question my family?"

Despite her disagreeable manner, there was something sad about the way her fingers, all of whose nails had been chewed down to the quick, clutched another one of her exquisite teacups. Especially since I gathered it wasn't filled with tea. Was she drinking from worry? Or guilt? John said Sharon never told a consistent story for where she was when Danny was hit. Though some part of me wanted to leave this unhappy woman alone with her troubles, I kept hammering at her.

"Look," I admitted, "I'm a pest. I know that. I never give up on anything. If I did, I'd never win races. Believe me, you'll tell me the truth now, or you'll tell me later. But you will tell me."

Finally, she snapped, "Okay, you win. I'm tired of lying, anyway. You wanna know where I was? At the Bed-a-Bye Motel—that's one of those dumps they rent by the hour." I was guessing she hadn't been alone. "Do you love him?"

The withering look she gave me made me feel about two years old. "What I love is being with a man who doesn't need to control every aspect of my life."

This was getting way too ugly, too much like my own family had been. It made me want to walk away, as much as the idea of Danny's injuries had. But I couldn't. As nice as he seemed, John Bricker was part of this twisted bunch; he couldn't challenge them. The cops wouldn't.

Zoe, I thought, it comes down to you.

* * *

John told me where to find Rudy West, whom he described as Eton's only real friend. Approaching the park near the beach that drug dealers frequented, I began to wonder about that friendship. This park didn't seem the kind of place for a slow, overweight boy to hang out. Were the Brickers just too involved with their own lives, and their perfect son, to spare a thought to the imperfect one?

Rudy West fit his surroundings: Collar-length hair unacquainted with shampoo, gang clothes, giant-sized chip on his shoulder and a minuscule soul apparent in his muddy brown eyes. To my surprise, he spoke quite freely to me.

"Yeah, Pepe showed me and Eat how to cut the car sideways when you pull out. In case . . . you're in a hurry."

When stealing cars? The handyman gave the little twerps a crash course.

"Leaves some cool rubber on the road," Rudy added.

"And Eton practiced?"

Rudy kicked at the crusty dirt beneath his feet with an Air Jordan big enough to house a family of five. "Yeah, some."

I asked where Eton had been Danny had been hit.

"He was out somewheres, running an errand," Rudy said. "I think he got lost or somethin'. Said the directions were wrong, even though his dad printed out the map from the Internet."

I used those map websites to generate my own directions to new places. Generally, I preferred the ones that decorated their maps with fun driving images, but none of them had ever failed me. "This errand—was it for you?"

"For his mom," he shot back.

"Even though they're twins, there seems to have been quite a difference between Danny and Eton. How did Eton feel about his superlative brother?"

The look he directed at me made me want to check my eye for spit.

"How would you?" Rudy asked.

Was that really what this crime was about? Had that slow, overweight boy, maybe feeling neglected by his mother and tired of being compared to his more dazzling twin, taken out his frustration on his brother using the tools Pepe Morales provided?

Three days a week Eton attended tutoring sessions after school. I had planned to catch him before the tutoring started, but I spent more time with Rudy than I thought, and it was late when I arrived at the school. I chained my bike to a post on the fringe of the parking lot and jogged across it toward the entrance.

Without warning, the blue Toyota Tercel John told me the twins shared came barreling across the high school parking lot at me. Only reflexes honed by competition saved my life. I hurled myself on the hood of a parked car. I thought the Tercel would crash into it. But the driver agilely cut it to the side and brought it to a stop, just as Pepe Morales had taught him. The door flew open, and a large boy, who looked like Danny Bricker would have if he'd been filled with air, hurled himself at me. He threw me back against the windshield of the car I'd taken refuge on. He pressed his forearm against my throat and leaned with all the might in that heavy body.

"Leave us alone!" he grunted. "Can't . . . take anymore."

I pushed against that giant form with all my strength. But while my body is honed for considerable endurance, I'm not a big woman, and I didn't have a fraction of the adrenaline coursing rough my veins as that boy did. Spots began to appear before my eyes.

Despite the hour, the noise Eton created drew a number of students and teachers from the school. Two male teachers pulled the boy away from me. When they let him go, I cringed, expecting him to leap back at me. To my surprise, he collapsed on the ground, in tears.

I rubbed my throat. "Knowing he's tight with that little thug, Rudy West, isn't such a surprise now," I muttered to myself.

One boy just snorted. "Yeah, right."

The police sirens severed that conversation. The cops took in my wounded throat, the sobbing boy, and the signature Morales cutaway on the pavement, and they took Eton in for questioning.

Two days later, Lou told me Eton Bricker was charged with the attempted murder of his twin brother.

* * *

I didn't hear from John. What did I expect? He may have asked for the truth, but that didn't mean he wouldn't resent the messenger.

My gut still tightened when I stopped into Danny's room

at the hospital. Seeing him there, as still as death, just made me itch to move. To prove I could?

The bright silver framed photos of the tarnished family were still rigidly arranged on the nightstand, but I didn't see the exquisite tea set anywhere. I found the pieces at last at the bottom of the wastepaper basket, crushed to bits. How fitting.

I slipped away to the nurses' station and questioned the male nurse I found there about Danny's future.

"The longer he hangs in there, the better his chances are," he said.

With an impatient sigh, I said, "I meant his chance of ever competing again."

The nurse just shook his head. I felt weak in the knees, for Danny, for me. I just hoped the roots on his needs weren't as deep as my own.

Because I never know when to quit, I'm always closure-deficient. Finally, I went to the Bricker house. Sharon was moving out, judging by the overstuffed suitcase she dragged out the door.

"Haven't you done enough to us?" she spat. "You destroyed our family."

I hadn't really. I just tugged at the Joker and their house of cards collapsed. But I didn't defend myself.

"You know what the worst part is?" Sharon demanded. "You still don't know how wrong you are. Eat would never have done that to Danny. Sure, he gets frustrated when he can't do things as well. But Eton loves Danny, not just because they're twins, but because Danny is everything that Eton wants to be."

She climbed into her car without thanking me for my efforts on her family's behalf. "Tell John he doesn't need to lock his den anymore," she threw over her shoulder.

I thought about the stupid things people use as excuses when relationships die. Things that didn't matter when they worked.

I spotted John through the open doorway. He was just standing in the entry, looking around. At what was left of his life? But he joined me at the door, and he refused my muttered apology with a toss of his hand.

"My choice. I knew you would learn the truth," he said.

"I saw you once in a race Danny competed in."

"Did I win?"

He laughed. "Of course. I don't think I've ever seen any-one as determined as you were."

That's me, obsessed to the end.

John hesitated. "I needed to know, for Danny's sake. But I wish I didn't."

Uncomfortable with my role in the operation, I changed the subject. "I saw Sharon's tea set broken at the hospital."

"She threw those pieces when she heard about Eat's ar-rest. She'll be sorry about it when she calms down. About a lot of things."

John had to leave, so I walked him to his car in the drive-way. I mounted my bike, only I remembered I drank all the water in my bottle on the ride over there.

"Can I fill my water bottle from your garden hose be-fore I leave?" I asked.

"Sure, it's around the back of the house. Just go through the gate."

I waved when he drove off and walked to the backyard. I found an amber hose at the rear of the house neatly coiled in a terracotta container, and silently gave thanks that the only area my own compulsive nature didn't extend into was my housekeeping. John did seem a little anal, but was that enough to break up a marriage? Maybe Sharon was one of those people who blame others for her mistakes.

I turned on the water, but since the hose rested in direct sunlight, it was warm. I pointed the nozzle into a bed of coral geraniums and let it run, while I stared through the sliding glass door next to the faucet into what must have been John's den. The surface of the heavy mahogany desk wasn't as neat as I'd expect. Stacked in the center was a messy pile of sheets of paper and different sized photographs.

The water finally ran cold, and I turned my attention to filling my water bottle. But something about the cartoon graphics I'd seen on the papers on John's desk gnawed at me. I looked again at the stack on the desktop, and tried to understand why those things troubled me.

When the answer hit me, the bottle slipped from my hand. Cold water splashed against my bare calves below my black Lycra bike shorts, but I scarcely noticed.

I pressed my face to the window, studying the various versions of the graphics I saw peaking out from the stack of pages, and the subjects of the date-stamped photos, and more importantly, how far back the dates went.

Once I saw how it all fit together, I knew I'd been played for every kind of a fool.

* * *

Time came to weigh on me. I knew if I was right, I had to get away from there. I'd noticed the house across the street was empty, and that a high hedge shielded part of the property from view.

I grabbed my bike and hid behind that hedge, and waited. If my fears were right, I knew it wouldn't take John long to realize his mistake. By locking the door to his den, he kept the items on his desk from those inside the house—but everything was visible to anyone standing outside that window. And he told me where to find the hose. If my conclusions were wrong, I could be waiting behind that hedge for a long time. If they weren't—

Before I could complete that thought, John's car careened into the driveway and jerked to a halt. He threw the door open and ran to the front door. He wasn't inside that long. When he returned, he'd put on a black windbreaker over his blue sport shirt. And he clutched a brown paper grocery bag, which had been rolled down to tightly contain a rectangular object around the size of the stack of papers and pictures I'd seen on his desk.

His car backed into the street in a rush. I watched him lay rubber in an effort to make a quick getaway from his quiet residential neighborhood. Much the way Pepe Morales did when he stole a car. I let him get a good lead, then took off after him on my bike.

If he hopped on the freeway, I was screwed. But if he stayed to surface streets, I might luck out. Traffic lights would keep him from gaining too much ground on me, and there are always too many cyclists on San Diego's streets for him to notice any one of them.

The gods were with me. Though John's Mercedes led me on a long, circuitous route, he finally parked his car in a strip mall adjacent to the sprawling Tecolate Natural Park, a wild preserve in central San Diego. Still clutching his brown bag, John picked up a trail and headed off into the park.

I stood at the trailhead until I lost sight of him in the undergrowth. I followed behind slowly on my bike, grateful for whatever impulse made me switch to my rugged mountain bike today and abandon my flimsy road bike, which I'd been using all week. The rutted trail dipped and rose, though overall climbed to a steep peak.

While he'd taken the time to don a windbreaker that seemed unnecessary in the balmy spring air, he hadn't changed from his loafers. They made him slip so many times, I came to recognize from a distance the little puffs of dust he would kick up when he fell. Despite his slips and falls, John stuck to his climbing trail, passing up plenty of chances to switch to less challenging and more crowded hiking trails that would take him lower into the canyon.

His steps slowed when he reached a clearing ringed by trees at the top of the hill. I stepped from my bike and waited some distance away to see what he would do. He leaned against a tree and caught his breath for a few moments. Then he found a large metal trashcan, and he rolled it into the center of the clearing. Reaching into his windbreaker, he brought out a can of charcoal lighter and a book of matches. He gave the trashcan a spritz of fluid and set it on fire.

I started to rest my bike against a tree, knowing I could approach more quietly on foot. But I'd make better getaway time on the bike. I centered the tires on the trail, where they would make less noise, and approached a cluster of trees at the edge of the clearing.

After watching the fire grow, John picked up the bag he'd put aside while lighting it. Just before he dropped it into the burning trash, I walked my bike into the clearing. "Throw the bag to the ground, John. It's over," I said.

He did drop the bag down, but only because I startled him. "Zoe, what—"

"You almost pulled it off. But the date-stamped photos of the Bed-a-Bye Motel prove you knew about Sharon's affair. And those graphics you copied from the Maps 'R' Us website—you used them to fake the map that sent Eton out on a wild goose chase. While you took your own van, and, with the flourish you learned for Pepe Morales, ran into Danny."

He must have discovered his wife had slipped the harness months ago. It enraged him so, he devised a plan to kill one of her sons and frame the other for it. I wondered how much he paid Rudy West to pose as Eton's friend and lead me astray.

But John wasn't perfect. Danny hadn't died. No wonder he spent so much time at his son's bedside; he couldn't allow the kid to tell the story if he ever came out of the coma. Then the police glommed onto the driving maneuver his handyman had taught him, and it seemed Sharon's life, while badly damaged, wouldn't be as thoroughly destroyed as he wanted.

"Sharon didn't do justice to how controlling you really are," I added.

Though the roaring fire brightened his face, John's steely eyes darkened. Yet he said nothing.

"The mistake you made was trying to make me your dupe," I said. "You only saw me on the race course. There, it's true, I never deviate from the course. In life, I play hop-scotch."

But not often enough. It pained me to admit how close he came to being right about me. Because of my single-minded nature, I followed the trail he'd left for me with relentless determination. If not for that fluke sighting of the evidence, I would never have seen the truth. Yet I should have known when I saw Sharon's teapot and cups in Danny's room. Those pieces weren't merely broken, they'd been crushed to dust. It took real hatred to do that.

"You blew it, you miserable cretin," I said.

I thought he would grab for the bag and try to burn it when he realized it was over, and I prepared myself to rush him. But he surprised me. The lighter fluid wasn't the only thing he'd slipped into the windbreaker while he was in the house.

He pulled an automatic from his jacket and pointed it at me. "Don't do the victory lap yet, bitch."

"You won't kill me," I said with more bravado than I felt. "There are too many people in the park. You couldn't get away with it."

An ugly smile crawled across John's face. "You're assuming that getting away with it is my objective now. It means more to me to make you pay for ruining my plans."

He aimed the gun at my pelvis, and then at my knees. My insides went cold. That threat I did believe. Robbing me of my ability to compete athletically fit his controlling nature. My heart began to throb erratically, my vision blurred. I couldn't face what he threatened to do to me.

John continued to sight the gun on different parts of my anatomy. "You see, Zoe, when you go out for revenge, you always need to size up the other guy's vulnerabilities. With Sharon, it's her kids. For you, it's your sport. Not such an Ironman now, are you?"

I was a heartbeat away from whimpering, from begging, promising him anything if he would spare me. Only my voice seemed to have locked along with my pathetic body. I always counted on my single-minded focus to allow me to leave my demons in my dust. Instead, that unrelenting need delivered me to them.

Worst of all, I would live a life without the things that gave it meaning—knowing I was too weak to fight for them. What was the point of achieving maximum fitness of the body, if my soul couldn't face the one challenge that mattered?

Zoe, what's it gonna be?

With no warning to John or myself, I leaped on my bike. I aimed my front tire at the burning trashcan. When the tire met the can, I used it to push the can forward until I had thrust it against John. That action threw his arms out, and the gun flew off into the bushes, but I didn't even look to see where it went. I just kept the pressure on the can, until I had pinned John between a large tree and that fire breathing monster.

While he screamed for the mercy he hadn't shown anyone in his family, I rallied my considerable strength and my obsessive will, and I kept him pinned in that position, until the heat threatened to melt his flesh.

Eventually, he stumbled free of my grasp. The burns had weakened his legs, however, and he tripped to the canyon's edge and tumbled over the side.

He landed somewhere well below, and while he alternatively begged and ordered me to help him, I just safeguarded the bag of evidence and lamented the destruction of a perfectly good tire.

Eventually, a hiker happened by, who wasn't quite that determined to get away from it all as hikers usually are, judging by his Banana Republic attire and the cell phone pressed to his ear. I broke into his conversation long enough to ask him to summon the cops.

John's burns were pretty bad, and despite Lou's intervention, the posse took me in for questioning. It took a while to sort out, but they released me later that day, and Eton the next. Now John recuperated down the hall from Danny's room, with round-the-clock police guards at the door.

Since that day, I spent a lot of time with Danny, holding his hand, talking to him. I tried to see him now, not as a symbol of some fear I couldn't face, but as a fallen comrade who deserved my support. Sometimes I relieved Sharon in the vigil she felt free to maintain, now that John was gone, and sometimes I just sat alongside her. We talked a lot, too, having both been manipulated in different ways by the same controlling man. By the deadly side of obsession.

After combing through the replacement china warehouses, I found matches for the teapot and teacups John had destroyed. Sharon said that too much had happened to her family to care about some china pieces. But I disagreed. It's important to put things right, even if only in the smallest ways. Sometimes, when we sipped tea together in those cups, we could almost forget what John did to the ones he promised to love.

I also took Eton running most days, so he could lose enough weight to finally shed his awful nickname. It was hard for me, running at his slow pace. But I had to admit he saw things that I missed when I streaked through life. He didn't mind sharing them, either.

No, I hadn't changed all my stripes—I was still a tiger on the race course. But I was trying to be less of one in life. Besides, it seemed only fair that I do what I could to help heal those people, after helping to tear their lives apart. Especially since, all the while I was healing them, they were healing me, too.

Kris Neri:

Kris Neri has published more than forty-five short stories, two of which were Derringer Award winners. She also writes the Tracy Eaton mystery novels, *REVENGE OF THE GYPSY QUEEN*, an Agatha, Anthony and Macavity Award nominee, and *DEM BONES' REVENGE*.

Mrs. Millet and Mrs. Hark: CREAM PUFFS

by Margaret Searles

The tour bus rolled south on the freeway, carrying its load of theater-goers to see "Les Miserables" at the Pantages Theater in Hollywood. Margaret Millet and Judy Hark were celebrating an anniversary; it had been ten years since they met on just such a theater trip.

"Remember?" asked Mrs. Hark. "Evita? And we were the only ones by ourselves, so we sat together."

"Historic," Mrs. Millet said. "We've had some good times since, haven't we?" She was shorter, rounder, and eleven years younger than her friend, and it did her good to look at Judy Hark and know there was still life to be lived. Judy looked—elegant was the only word—in a crisp, black pants-suit, her candy-striped silk blouse pinned at the neck with an antique cameo. Her auburn hair was expertly coiffed, her nails freshly manicured. As always, she looked like *Somebody* and would get special treatment anywhere.

The bus had originated in Santa Porta and was nearly full when Mrs. Millet and Mrs. Hark got on in Gambol Beach. As the miles went spinning by, the two friends observed their tripmates with interest.

"See that couple on the left, about half way up?" Judy nodded toward them. "Obviously not married. She's all over him! But he looks bored and embarrassed."

"That's because they've had sex. He'd be all over her if they hadn't," Mrs. Millet said.

"Of course. Just like my first husband. Cute, isn't he? Face like a sad monkey."

The young couple were exceptions among passengers mostly of their own generation. The older women wore their hair short and curly, either frankly gray or tinted that dish-water-blonde shade that covers gray so well and is supposed to soften a wrinkled face. The men were hearty and talkative, or quiet and reluctant, as though they were doing something not quite manly to please their wives.

"By the way, guess what I brought," Mrs. Hark said.

Mrs. Millet had already noticed the quilted, insulated pouch Mrs. Hark carried in addition to her purse. "Let's see— chicken paprika? Banana Bread? Oh, don't tantalize me!" Margaret Millet did not cook, but appreciated her friends who did.

"Cream puffs."

"Cream puffs! Your own home-made? Oh boy, oh boy, oh boy!" Mrs. Millet knew Judy's cream puffs; walnut-sized miniatures of chewy pastry with a rich cream filling. Taken whole into the mouth and bitten, they flooded the taste buds with pleasure.

The massive coach sped down the California coast, slowed for Gaviota Pass and Santa Barbara, raced the traffic through Carpenteria, Ventura, Oxnard, Thousand Oaks, and geared down to grind over the hills into the San Fernando Valley.

Somewhere in North Hollywood, the bus suddenly swerved to the right, decelerated sharply, and stopped on the freeway shoulder. A chorus of gasps, exclamations, and "What are we stopping for?"s broke out among the passengers.

"Sorry folks," the driver said, "we're losing power, and I need to see why. We're early, so not to worry." He opened the bus door. Mrs. Millet looked at her watch: 12:33.

The young man with the affectionate girlfriend disengaged himself. "I'm a diesel mechanic. Maybe I can help." He followed the driver, and soon metallic noises came from the back of the bus.

"I'm sure it's just something minor," said Dolores Dell, their tour guide. "We're only twenty minutes from the Pantages, and the show doesn't start until two, so we've plenty of time."

"How does she know it's something minor?" snorted Mrs. Hark. "I'm glad Monkey Wrench, there, understands engines."

* * *

Young Ferdie Mentone spotted the bus from the frontage road nearby and parked the stolen car he was driving. What a target! The name scrolled along the side of the bus spoke to him: "Mother Lode Stages." A whole bus full of rich trippers—this could be his own personal gold mine!

Ferdie had lived for eighteen unsheltered years. Smart and funny, his irregular features formed a marvelously expressive face. He had nothing but scorn for suckers who stayed in school or worked at menial jobs. A clever thief, he saw no reason why the "more fortunate" shouldn't supplement his mother's waitress work. A dare-devil, but not a violent boy, Ferdie disliked fights. Fights were stupid and spoiled your good looks.

He now inspected the gun Honest John had given him. The "Saturday Night Special" looked deadly enough. People folded right up when he pointed the thing at them. Ferdie waited.

* * *

The driver poked his head into the bus and called, "Bad fan belt, folks. I may have a spare. If so, we'll be back on the road in a few minutes. If not, we're right by a call box. We'll get you to the show. Just bear with us."

No spare fan belt. At 1:00 P.M. Dolores Dell reported, "Edmund called in, and we should be rescued in just a little while. We still have plenty of time to get to the theater, so don't worry."

Getting out of the bus was impossible. The freeway traffic sped by; freight trucks pushing great blasts of air that made the bus sway, a constant stream of cars that went woosh, woosh, woosh, punctuated by the staccato roar of an occasional motorcycle.

At 1:35 Dolores Dell announced, "The repair truck should be here any minute now. I figure we'll get to the theater about five minutes late. That won't be too bad. Yes, we should be about five minutes late." She passed out sandwiches, cold drinks, and cross-word puzzles for their entertainment.

The air conditioning, of course, had died with the engine. Passengers propped the bus windows open at the bottom, letting in air, soot, and noise. The lavatory, just behind the seat shared by Mrs. Millet and Mrs. Hark, became very popular. Two o'clock—curtain time—passed with no comment from driver or guide.

Mrs. Hark fretted, "Why don't they *do* something! It's been over an hour since they called, and I haven't even seen a Highway Patrol car!" She added, "Do have another cream puff, Margaret." The cream puffs—miniature pockets of ambrosia—were their chief consolation.

At 3:30, mutiny seemed imminent, and the driver had to act. "Folks, I want to thank you for being such good sports.

The engine has cooled off, so I'm going to take a chance and drive to the first off-ramp. We can at least get to a regular telephone. Please close all the windows, and we'll give it a try."

He walked through the bus, making sure the lever marked "Emergency Exit" was firmly clamped at the bottom of each window, then started the engine and eased onto the freeway. The passengers cheered.

* * *

Ferdie Mentone started his engine, too. This had been worth waiting for! His eyes sparkled, and when the bus turned down the Tujunga Avenue off-ramp and stopped beside a laurel hedge, half a block from Moorpark Street, Ferdie laughed out loud. He parked around the corner, slipped on his ski mask, and trotted up to the bus, gun in hand.

The bus door opened. Dolores Dell met Ferdie Mentone's gun, backed by Ferdie Mentone's masked head and lean wiry body. She yelped and froze, eyes bulging, mouth open, clip board crashing in the gutter.

"Back in the bus, lady!" Ferdie turned her around with one arm and jabbed the gun painfully in her ribs. "Okay guys, anybody moves, she gets it." His voice squeaked a little from excitement.

One of the dishwater-blondes screamed, and her husband grabbed her hand. Monkey Wrench's emotional girlfriend flung herself around him like a straight jacket. Mrs. Hark ducked low in her seat and hastily stowed her diamond ring in a crack.

Ferdie spotted a waste basket beside the driver. "Empty that," he snapped. "Dump it! Put it right here!"

Edmund, his face ghastly, complied and then slumped back behind the wheel.

"You people come up, *one at a time*, and put your wallets and goodies in here. You first, lady, and don't forget that pretty watch. Now get back to your seat!"

Ferdie's heart raced. Gloriously high, he grinned behind his ski mask. Look at these putty-faced wrinklers jump to please him! Funniest thing he'd ever seen. Keep the cash and take the rest to Honest John—guess he'd get a little respect, after this. The Great California Stage Coach Robbery! Aha, Zorro!

For long minutes it seemed he was right. The scene was too far from the shops and restaurants of Moorpark Street for pedestrians. Passing drivers saw only a bus full of people. One at a time, the travelers stumbled up the aisle, deposited their valuables in the waste basket, and returned to their seats. If they had ideas of heroism, Dolores Dell's obvious terror changed their minds. Her high-piled black hair writhed like Medusa's as she nodded and whispered, over and over, "Do as he says. Do as he says."

But Ferdie Mentone hadn't allowed for Ms. Caroline Priddy, age 83, who lived in an apartment behind the laurel hedge. His world contained no one like Caroline Priddy. With no idea of the robbery in progress, she saw the disabled bus and wanted to help. She was curious, too, and would satisfy her curiosity while she offered the use of her telephone, bathroom, or whatever was needed.

Mrs. Hark saw her coming, a brisk, erect little party in a lavender sweater and flowered skirt, with hair the color of a ripe peach. It looked as though she would walk right into the robber's activities.

Levering open the bottom of her window, Mrs. Hark stuck out a hand. "Pssst! Go back! We're being robbed!"

Ms. Priddy did not go back; she came closer, not sure she had heard correctly. "Can I help you folks? What's wrong?"

Thankful for the two dozen passengers between her and the robber's ski-masked eyes, Mrs. Hark repeated as loudly as she dared, "We're being robbed! Up front—he's got a gun!"

"Robbed! How perfectly *dreadful!*" Ms. Priddy was outraged. "Should I call the police? No, they'd never get here in time." She shook herself and squared her shoulders—no bandit could intimidate *her*—and marched toward the front of the bus, heedless of Mrs. Hark's efforts to stop her.

Inside the bus, Monkey Wrench moved up the aisle (it was his turn to enrich the waste basket), and his ladyfriend, unable to stay alone in her seat, came right behind him.

Outside, Caroline Priddy reached up to Ferdie's back, prodded his spine with her bony forefinger, and said sharply, "What are you doing! Stop it this instant!"

Completely surprised, Ferdie lurched sideways (he

would surely have shot Dolores Dell if the gun had been loaded) and turned his head. For Dolores, this was the final shock. She fainted, an inert, 150 pound weight in Ferdie's arms. He staggered backward on the step, Monkey Wrench tackled the pair of them waist-high, and Ms. Priddy stepped aside just in time to avoid being on the bottom, as they tumbled out of the bus. The pistol went flying.

Driver Edmund came to life, barged out and grabbed up the gun. Waving it recklessly, he started giving orders. "Call the police! Hold him—don't let him get away! Stand back, everybody!"

Before Monkey could get a firm grip, Ferdie squirmed out from under Dolores, pushed Caroline Priddy aside, and ran through the block like a track star. Mrs. Hark had a good view of his back as he cleared the hedge.

Edmund yelled, "Stop!" and pointed the impotent gun, but he made no attempt at pursuit. His pot belly still blocked the bus door, too, not that anyone else wanted to chase the robber. The passengers were all too busy diving for their belongings in the waste basket.

Monkey got up gasping for breath, and his ladyfriend squeezed out of the bus and threw herself into his arms, nearly knocking him down again. Dolores groaned and tried to rise.

"We must call the police," Caroline Priddy said, taking charge. "Come along, dear. You need restoratives." She pointedly ignored Edmund and shepherded Dolores toward her front door.

At the back of the bus, Mrs. Hark retrieved her diamond ring and said, "That's a remarkable woman, Margaret. Let's go use her telephone and see if we can find a way to get home. I don't know about you, but I've had enough."

* * *

And what of Ferdie Mentone? He burned. His marvelous hold-up bombed by a little old lady! And he'd lost his "piece"—what if it could be traced to Honest John? The car didn't matter, he had "borrowed" it from the May Company parking lot, but losing the gun was serious. What if this business got into the papers? If Honest John found out that he, Ferdie, had blown such a chance—it didn't bear thinking about.

Brooding on these matters and nursing his lumps and

scrapes, Ferdie caught a transit bus to central Hollywood and got off at the Greyhound Depot. This might be a very good time to visit his sister in Oxnard. Her husband was a foreman at Oxnard Farms; maybe he'd offer Ferdie a job. Time to lie low? disappear? give up crime? Ferdie no longer felt like Zorro—he felt like an eighteen year old kid who had gone too far.

                              * * *

Mrs. Hark learned that the northbound Greyhound would leave the North Hollywood depot at 5:45; they could call a cab and catch it, easily.

Caroline Priddy objected. "Oh, no, I can take you to the bus station. It will only take a minute to get my car out." She grabbed a purse, saying, "I've had my afternoon cocktail, so I'll be extra careful."

A few minutes later, Ms. Priddy let the grateful ladies out at the bus station and drove away, waving off their fervent thanks.

"Restores your faith in human nature, doesn't she," Mrs. Hark remarked, clutching the bag that still contained a few cream puffs.

"I will live in a house by the side of the road and be a friend to man," Mrs. Millet quoted. "I got her address. We ought to send flowers."

They entered the cramped, dirty store-front that passed for a bus depot in North Hollywood. A row of hard wooden seats faced the grubby ticket counter. A few people waited, mostly Mexican farm workers and young servicemen with boot-camp haircuts, going home on leave. The ladies drew together, feeling out of place in this company.

They bought tickets, and soon the bus rolled up outside, nearly filled with passengers from Los Angeles and Hollywood, including Ferdie Mentone. Without his ski mask, he was just another boy to Mrs. Millet and Mrs. Hark, as they took seats across the aisle from him.

Mrs. Hark took a cream puff and passed the pouch to Mrs. Millet who popped one of the rich, comforting morsels into her mouth. How sustaining! The lad across the aisle gave her a hungry grin and, because he had such an engaging face, she handed him the bag. His grin got wider. "Thanks," he said.

Darkness fell, and it started to rain. When Ferdie got off the bus in Oxnard, he handed back the cream puff bag with an angelic smile. Mrs. Hark saw him from the rear as he sprinted into the depot. His back looked vividly familiar.

"Look, Margaret! Oh, but it can't be! Lots of boys wear jeans and athletic jackets."

Two hours later, the Greyhound bus stopped in Gambol Beach where Mrs. Millet's pickup truck waited, gleaming wetly under the street lights.

After Mrs. Millet saw Judy safely through her front door, she turned the truck toward home, her mind playing back portions of the day. What a day! Thank goodness for the initiative of Judy Hark—when will the others ever get home? . . . The tour people will have to give us our money back . . . Wonder what *Les Miserables* was like . . . supposed to be about the Desperate Poor—like our robber? and the people in that bus depot?

Then, as she pulled into her own carport, she saw the cream puff bag; Judy had forgotten it. My, those cream puffs were good. Better take the bag inside—she could return it filled with—a nice mystery paperback?—some little thing to show her appreciation.

Indoors, Mrs. Millet opened the bag in case it held one more cream puff. No, they were all gone—but the bag was not empty. A bit of dark wool lay at the bottom, like somebody's knitting. She pulled it out and turned it in her hands. How odd! And then she saw what it was. But why? For a sign—a promise to change? Or just a tease? She'd never know, but she could hope.

Ferdie had taken the last cream puff—and left his ski mask in the bag.

Margaret Searles:

Margaret Searles is an ex-chemist, -teacher, and -book-store owner. Her stories and articles have been published in *Whispering Willow*, *Sleuthhound* (contest winner), *Futures* (Fire To Fly Award), *Mordsweiber* (in German), *Mystery Readers Journal*, the *SLO Death* Anthologies, *New Times*, and other publications. She edits fiction and holds memberships in Oregon Writers Colony and Sisters in Crime (Treasurer, California Central Coast Chapter). "Cream Puffs," the very first story she wrote about Mrs. Millet & Mrs. Hark, won the Publisher's Choice Award when it appeared in *Futures Magazine*. Four complete novels starring these Senior Sleuths are now looking for a publisher.

LOWBALL

by Gary Phillips

Sweat collected in his goatee, and Monk could feel the stuff gather along the rim of his collar. A heavyset white guy sported out in lime green suspenders, the upper portion of his shirt wet, munched on a pear in the corner. Near him, a water fountain leaked coolant. There were only three people sitting in the oppressive atmosphere of the lunch room. Everyone else was outside eating on the lawn and at lunch tables.

"The police said I should forget it. My husband was killed for $73, it happens every day, they said." The room's humidity didn't bother Betty Patrick. She had more important matters to contend with. "I don't want to forget it, Ivan."

Monk shifted his gaze from her to the beefy man in the corner then back. Betty's fellow worker seemed genuinely immersed in the Super Bowl highlights edition of the Sports Illustrated he was leafing through.

"I hate to sound like Larry Elder, Betty, but you and I both know meaningless death can be too much of life in South Central L.A."

A tiny smile eased the tension on her handsome face. "I know." Her eyes fixed on him and they were like twin pieces of hardened amber. There was a resolve mirrored in them, and there was no letting it go.

"Marcus is coming home from work after an overtime shift on Friday night," Monk began, hoping to show her how hopeless it was by going over it again. "He stops at a liquor store to get a six-pack and also buys three Lotto tickets." She nodded. "He leaves with his beer, rounds the corner where his car is parked, and is shot. No witnesses, no apparent motive other than a stick-up." He closed his steno pad.

Betty Patrick touched Monk's arm. "We were married for eight years. Had no children because we were saving our money to put something down on a house. Marcus and I had been sweethearts since our junior year when I transferred to Locke High."

There was no pleading or wheedling in her voice. Just the finality of a woman who wanted some reason in a chaotic universe. The bell rang signaling an end to the half-hour lunch the employees of Tycor Brake Company received each day. The young widow rose but didn't leave as the man in the suspenders exited.

"I have over nine thousand in the bank. I've got nothing to spend it on now, Ivan. I can pay you your rate for whatever you can find. The police figure it's just one more young black man in a never ending assembly line of them snuffed out in the low level genocide we practice on one another daily. Solving his murder is not a priority with the law, but it is with me."

A supervisor stuck his head in the room then withdrew it at a withering look from Betty. She went on, "Reverend Tompkins gave me your name, he's the pastor of my . . . my mother-in-law's church. He did the service. He said you were to be counted among the wheat, not the chaff."

Now it was Monk's turn to smile. "Okay, Betty, I'll take a run at it." He got up and shook her hand. "I'm not promising anything."

"I understand," she said gratefully.

He walked with her onto the shop floor toward the work bench where she assembled truck calipers. "I'd like to swing by your apartment around seven to go through your husband's things and drop off a contract."

"Good, I'll see you then." She returned to her duties and Monk got into his restored '64 Galaxie parked on the lot. He left the industrial city of Vernon (population some 10,000 by day and less than 300 actual residents at night) and got to his office in Culver City in less than thirty minutes.

Sitting at his antique Colonial desk, he dialed Wilshire Division and got his only cop friend, Detective Lieutenant Marasco Seguin, on the line.

"Home deduction," Monk said.

"Hollywood Dick, what up?" Seguin drawled in that unique inflection of his. A combination of East Los Vato and professor.

"Make a call for me to the Southwest Division and put

in a sterling recommendation to the cops handling the Marcus Patrick killing. I'd like to know what they've found out so far."

"Quires?"

"Because I gave you a good tip which helped you break a murder case you took the credit for a couple of weeks ago."

"Well hell, if you're going to be that way," Seguin laughed. "Hang by the phone for a bit, I'll see what I can do."

The connection severed and Monk re-read the notes he'd made at his meeting with Betty Patrick. The late Marcus Patrick had worked at Academy Litho in Gardena as a computer film separator. The man drank socially, not to excess, played poker now and then with a group of friends, and fixed the leaky faucets around the house. The couple lived in a duplex on Van Buren, and used to get out to the movies or a club maybe once a month. Betty Patrick knew he wasn't in debt to any gambler, and was positive her husband hadn't been robbed by a prostitute as one of the cops had suggested to her.

Monk looked at the next page in his note pad and saw where he'd written that the liquor store was across the street from a quickie motel. But it did seem that angle on the crime was wrong. Prostitutes or their pimps had been known to rob a customer, but usually when they were in a more compromising situation.

Sitting and waiting, Monk puffed on a Jose Marti torpedo and spun various theories around in his head. If you discounted the obvious, that it was a common but tragic random street crime, then it was planned. After all, the robber had taken the wallet, but not the watch nor the gold band on Patrick's finger. Of course the thief might have just been in a hurry.

Maybe Patrick was working with a printer who was counterfeiting and got bumped off by his partner. Monk liked that idea and wrote it down. Or maybe Patrick was having an affair. The picture Betty gave him showed a sharp featured, muscular man. Counting their time with each other in high school, they'd been together nearly eleven years. Yeah, he could have gotten the itch. Jealous boyfriend or the girlfriend herself shoots the philandering husband and makes it look like a robbery.

Monk looked at the list of the late man's friends. If he was fooling around, one of them was sure to know. Man had to brag to his running buddies about gettin' some on the side. Monk reflected on his own relationship with his long-time girlfriend, Judge Jill Kodama. Before he could dwell on such matters too long, the phone rang.

It was a detective named McClane assigned to the Patrick murder. He was curt but answered Monk's questions. From the cop Monk got nothing new except the names of the managers of the New Experience Motel, and the owners of the liquor store. McClane abruptly ended their call with the pat "If you dig up anything, let me know."

The New Experience Motel was on south Hoover near Vernon. It was a graffitied yellow and black cinder block low slung wonder. Two women, one black, the other Latina, and both dressed in outfits even Frederick's of Hollywood would find risque, traded jokes with each other in front of the joint. Monk parked across the street in front of Diamond Star Liquors and went inside the store.

"No man," Wilcox, the co-owner of the establishment, said to him and the twenty on the counter.

"You didn't see or hear anything, huh?" Monk asked.

Wilcox, an older black man in starched white shirt and pressed khakis stared blank faced at Monk. "Look here, I've been running this business for thirty-two years. Two riots, several earthquakes, do-rag wearin' gangbangers and them no-smilin' Koreans ain't put me out of business yet. And the reason is because I don't worry myself in the affairs of my fellow man." With that, he put his back to the money, Monk, and the world, and continued setting his bottles in order.

Monk walked over to the motel. The two women were gone, no doubt having acquired some five minute company. He went to the closed-in booth with the word 'MANIGER' incorrectly spelled out in press-on letters forming a crooked line across its heavy glass. A curtain of dark material loomed behind the glass, and a thin Indian woman appeared from around it.

She shoved a registration card and a stubby pencil at Monk through the space at the bottom of the glass. Monk put the twenty into the metal recess beneath the slot. "I'd like to ask you some questions about the shooting that happened across the street three weeks ago."

She considered the bill then said, "What shooting?"

Monk added another twenty.

Her hand descended on the money like it was manna. "All I heard that night was the shot, then a car leaving in a hurry. Same as I told the cops." The forty was snatched up.

"See what kind of car it was?"

"No, no, didn't see." She turned to go back behind the curtain.

"You only heard one shot?"

"Yes, yes." She went away.

A door to a room opened, and Monk turned to see the Latina who'd been out front stroll onto the courtyard. She was young and pretty, but the cynical cast of one who plied her trade in human loneliness was already distorting her features. She walked past where he stood, her mini-skirt hiked high over one of her hips. She gave Monk the eye as a middle-aged white man also emerged from the room, then scurried off to his late model Thunderbird.

"Did you see anything the night of the shooting?" Monk asked the young woman, coming up alongside her as she lolled on the corner of the Experience.

"You ain't no cop, you're too cute." she said. Monk produced another twenty, holding the folded bill tight between his thumb and his hand balled into a fist. "I pay better than the cops."

"You mean the thing that went down 'bout a month ago at the liquor store?" She tilted her head to indicate the store across the street.

"That's right. Were you around that night?"

"What if I was? There some kind of reward being offered?"

Monk was inclined to lie, figuring she was just stringing him along. If she did know anything, probably McClane had already sweated her. Still. "If your information leads me to the killer, it could mean something substantial for you."

She puckered her red lips and her baby browns disappeared in slits. She seemed to be considering her answer when the black hooker walked up.

"If she's arguing price with you, big man, see about my

rates for dates." The second one said, placing a hand on Monk's arm and squeezing his triceps. "Goddamn, you work that iron steady, huh?"

The Latina pulled her friend over and whispered to her. Then she said, "You got a number, man?"

Monk gave her one of his cards. "Think about it. There's more than a twenty in it for you if you produce something of value." Yeah, a good citizen's award.

The black woman nodded at her friend. "Okay."

In the evening Monk went through the few artifacts representing the too-short life of Marcus Patrick. As he did, he asked the widow more about his habits and hobbies and took more notes. Afterward, he thanked her and went home.

His abode these days was a split-level overlooking the reservoir in Silverlake. The mortgage had Kodama's name on it, who was out of town at a conference until Sunday. The fact the house wasn't his bothered him less and less, particularly as they talked more and more about having children.

He dismissed fretting on the implications of that as he constructed two smoked turkey sandwiches, added a side of coleslaw, and a dark Becks for lubrication. Eating his meal, Monk watched C-SPAN which replayed an address by Senator Jesse Helms at a Heritage Foundation function. Helms was going on about the connection his researchers had uncovered between homosexuality and global warming.

* * *

Johnny Briggs nudged Howard Washington and laughed heartily. "Shit, Marc wasn't no macker. That boy was a square as a box of sugar cubes."

Washington drank more of the beer Monk had bought the two of them for lunch at the 5C's seafood restaurant on 54th Street. "Damned if that ain't so, brah. Marc might smack his lips at pussy same as all of us, but naw, he didn't dip his skeeter where it didn't belong."

"Yeah," Briggs agreed, "he wasn't no Cleavont."

The two laughed again then looked at each other. Washington said, "Don't mistake our foolin' around for what it ain't, Monk. We like to remember the good times with our friend, not the fact that some cowardly motherfuckah shot him down in the street."

"I understand. Who's Cleavont?" Monk signaled for the

waitress to bring two more beers.

Briggs' shoulders rose and fell. "Dude I know. He and I used to work over at the Greyhound depot in Santa Monica 'fore it closed. I invited him to a couple of our poker games and he's always goin' on about what chick he's doing.'"

"All talk and no fact," Monk said.

"Oh, I've met some of his honeys," Briggs said. "I guess it's fair to say he did most of what he said he did."

Monk talked more with the two, getting the names of other men Patrick and the two had played poker with on different occasions. Later, he called Briggs at his home and got their phone numbers and addresses.

As afternoon lengthened, Monk met Cleavont Derricks at his apartment off Stocker in the Crenshaw District.

He was large in the torso, slim in the hips. His do was done in an semi-Jheri Kurl forming oily ringlets of his dyed hair, and he wore too much cologne. Crow's feet were beginning to form in the corners of his bright eyes, and Monk had the impression as the years descended on him, they would not be welcome.

"No, Monk, I haven't got any idea who would off Patrick." From a CD outfit on a bookshelf, Anita Baker's voice soothed in the background. "I only talked with him at Johnny's."

"You two get to conversing about anything in particular?"

An imp's grin creased Derricks' smooth face. "Women and money, you know how it goes."

It went like that and over the next few days Monk talked to all the men who'd been involved in the poker games at Briggs' house. It was looking more like Betty Patrick would never have an answer.

Then he got a call from Marcy, the Latina hooker.

"Can you meet me down at the Experience tonight? room 4."

"What time?"

"Around seven." She hung up.

Monk knocked on the right door at the appointed time. The Indian woman was behind her glass, a box from Kentucky Fried Chicken at her elbow. She went back around her curtain quickly.

"Come on in, baby," she said sweetly, and he stepped

inside. Pain blossomed across the upper portion of his back and he staggered forward. Gritting his teeth, Monk sank to his knees as he dully heard the door slam shut.

A shadow contorted across the filthy shag carpet and Monk got his body around in time to see the round end of something plowing the air over his head. He got under the swing but the batter adjusted and brought the wood down on his shoulder.

"Yeah, motherfuckah," the man wielding the timber said. "Think you can come around her flashing money and my ho's not tell me?"

Monk blinked, compartmentalizing the pain as he sized up his opponent. The pimp was dressed in a tailored sport coat, open collar shirt, over-sized cotton shorts, no socks, tasseled shoes and a derby atop his small head. He was hefting an large wooden mallet like something Tom would chase Jerry with in one of their cartoons. He was an escapee from a Master P video.

The man began another attack but Monk buried a straight left into the other's stomach.

"Sheeit," he exhaled, doubling over.

Marcy, who'd been sitting on the edge of the bed, launched her body and landed on Monk's back. "Get him, Snow, get his money, baby."

Snow, darker than Monk, had his mouth agape like a tunnel, the mutant mallet held slack in his gloved hand.

Monk worked to get to his feet, but Marcy was punching him in the side. With her other hand she was yanking on his ear. He gripped her leg and spun his body, crashing down on top of her with force.

Marcy swore like a drill sergeant but Monk was already in motion and rolled off as Snow struck again with his weapon. The mallet smacked against Marcy's thigh with a mushy thud.

"Hey, watch it," she yelled.

"Shut up," Snow said, bringing the mallet back into play. He arced it again at Monk's head who was now back on his feet. But having anticipated such an action, Monk snatched up the room's sole chair to block the weapon's descent.

He shoved with the chair, getting his two hundred plus behind it. Snow's body cracked against the cheaply made door in the confining room. The pimp's head dipped down. Monk kicked him in the jaw. The derby flew off as the clean shaven head snapped back.

Monk looked down at Marcy, who was rubbing her bruised thigh.

"Big punk," she said in a little girl's whine.

"Sorry to spoil the surprise." Monk stepped over a groggy Snow sitting on the floor and picked up the mallet. Instinctively, the pimp covered his head with his arms.

Monk showed his teeth, and went out into the air carrying the thing. Gathering himself in the courtyard, he heard a familiar sound and looked across the street at the liquor store. He saw something he hadn't before and smiled.

* * *

He hit him hard alongside his head with the folded newspaper.

"Goddammit," the other man swore, wheeling around at Monk. Recognition tempered his anger. "What'd you do that for?"

Monk heard the wariness in the man's voice. "You know why," he snarled.

The other man sagged against the side of his van. "It's not like I meant to kill him." Workers filed past the two.

"Bullshit," Monk said.

He looked at him, searching for relief but there was none to give. "How'd you find out?"

"There're two Dumpsters rented by Diamond Star Liquors and a shop next to them. Every other Friday at 7:15 or thereabouts the truck comes to empty them. The driver remembered seeing your black and tan van that evening. The one I'd seen you drive up in when I took you and Johnny to lunch."

Howard Washington's head did a little movement. He looked way past where Monk was standing. "Nobody filled out a summer dress like Jenny. Only she looked on marriage as merely words on paper. She figured her beauty would make me so desperate for her, I'd keep letting anything slide."

A meanness crept into his voice, and it was clear Jenny stood before him in his mind. "One night I waited up for her. We had a place outside of Galveston where I worked at a boat yard. It wasn't much more than a fancy lean-to, but it was clean and comfortable. For two at least. She came in, hadn't even bothered to wash the smell of sex off of her."

Monk swallowed.

Washington went on, "She was high and passed out on the bed in her clothes. But I could see her panties were missing. I cleaved her head in two with a claw hammer and left her body on the edge of the interstate." The violence drained from him and a purity calmed his face.

"Nobody suspected you?"

"No. She had a couple of boyfriends who got the go-round but they were let go eventually. Sheriff figured some other dude she'd picked up had done it." He rubbed his chest like something burned inside of him. "She was part Seminole, man. She was beautiful."

Monk took Washington over to Southwest Station to make his statement to McClane. Pulling into a parking space on the street, Monk asked him, "Why'd you kill Patrick?"

"It was one of the few times we played poker at my crib. Afterwards, me and Marcus was the only ones left. We're both got a buzz on and we get to talkin' about women, you know how it gets."

"Sure," Monk said.

"I don't know how I got on to it, but he was talking about how he couldn't cheat on his old lady even if tempted by a stone fox. Said too it would kill him if Betty ever did it to him." He snorted at the irony.

Two uniforms passed along the sidewalk, staring at the two. No doubt assessing if they were wanted, Monk ruminated.

"For some reason, I told him. I guess I wanted some kind of understanding. Once I started, I couldn't stop. I told him how I'd put up with Jenny's foolin' around until I couldn't tolerate it any more." Washington wiped at his eyes. "She clowned me, man, over and over. Wasn't trying to be discrete about it, you know?"

They got out of the car. Washington's body stiffened as he took in the police station. Monk got sharp, but the other man compliantly marched forward.

"What did Patrick say when you told him?"

"Nothing. I mean he kind of looked at me then laughed.

I tried to make it a joke and said I wished I'd killed her."

"But it wouldn't leave you alone?" Monk wondered aloud. His hand was on the door handle.

The man plucked his lips with his fingers. "What if he got to thinking I wasn't foolin'. What if he made a call down to Galveston?"

Monk was pretty sure Patrick had rationalized Washington's confession as a sick joke. Otherwise, given how close they were, his widow would have mentioned it. "So you followed him from work that Friday night to kill him." They went inside. Civilians and uniforms moved about in pre-ordained patterns.

"No, man, that's not how it was," Washington pleaded.

"You had the gun on you," Monk said.

"I kept it in the glove box. Everybody's strapped in L.A. I'd worked myself up so bad over it I just had to talk to him." He paused, gnawing on his lip and kneading his knuckles. "The piece was in my hand without me thinking about it."

Yet he'd tried to make it look like a robbery, but Monk would let a jury decide how premeditated Washington's mind-set had been. The duo went to the front desk.

Washington worked his hands like he was molding clay. "I always knew women would do me in."

Monk's mouth was too dry for words.

Washington stared ahead then said. "Lowball. That was the last hand we played. Marc had a natural wheel: ace, deuce, three, four, five. He won big that night."

Later, Monk drove to Betty Patrick's house. He played a Muddy Waters cassette. "You're Gonna Miss Me" finished as he pulled into her driveway.

Gary Phillips:

Gary Phillips has written in several mediums, while mostly sober, and enjoys a good hand of poker now and then. Check out his website at: www.gdphillips.com for more of his work.

LEMON DROPS

by Susan M. Stephenson

"Look, John . . . That's crap! The supplier has got to be more responsive. We're talking business here, not what he 'feels like'—and business will be lost if he can't deliver. I suggest you make him understand that as simply and clearly as possible."

Kate Kemper felt the day pressing down on her already, though the battered office clock hadn't made it to 10:00 A.M. Trying to ignore the first signs of a headache, she barely noticed The Boss walk in with the latest new hire. Kate forced her attention back to the phone to cut off John's excuses. "We have product to get out the door. We have customers waiting. I won't have one flaky supplier damage our business with late or incomplete parts shipments. He signed a contract. That's all there is to it. If the guy wants to work on his screenplay, he does it on his own time!"

Slamming the receiver onto its cradle, she rested her elbows on the desk and rubbed her temples. This was not going to be a fun day. She could feel it. Or maybe it was just the Santa Anas getting to her. The company's aged air conditioning was beginning to wheeze from the strain of the heat building outside. She hated the grubby office in the grubby building in a grubby industrial section of North Hollywood.

"Kate, I'd like you to meet Charles Leimon," a raspy voice cut into her thoughts.

Startled, she looked up to see The Boss standing at her desk. The son of the ailing owner of the business, he filled the chair—but never the shoes—of his father. Next to The Boss a gangly man in his mid-twenties stood grinning with large yellowed teeth and no emotional warmth. "He's our new expediter."

"Welcome to the company." Extending her hand to be polite, Kate suppressed the chill down her back. The Boss's prize had one of those dead fish handshakes. Another loser, she thought. Where does he find them? Her phone rang, its shrill nagging a convenient excuse to cut the conversation off.

Lunch at a mini-mall Chinese restaurant meant braving the heat, but the change of scene was a tonic to the unending hassles of the workday. Mary Harris was waiting at a table when Kate arrived.

"Aah," Kate sighed, reaching for the menu she knew by heart, "This air conditioning feels wonderful!"

"Isn't yours working?" Mary looked cool and efficient, the soft sage color of her cotton knit dress setting off her scrubbed Irish looks.

"In this weather?" Kate grumbled. "It's barely keeping the office livable. The Boss, of course, has a new window unit, but the rest of us have to make do with the system that's ready for the Guinness Book." She knew her face was flushed, her hair straggling, and her dress limp. After days of building Santa Ana winds, the heat melts the soul. "I'll have the Chinese chicken salad," she told the waiter, "Lots of ice tea, please.

"Remember my supplier, the one who's such a flake? He's working on a screenplay! In his dreams he thinks he's going to sell it to Jean-Claude Van Damme or somebody, so he's turning out pages instead of turning out my parts," Kate shook her head. "I thought I'd heard it all . . ."

"Did you hear about the latest missing woman?" Anxiety brushed Mary's face.

"Another one?" Kate asked. "All I've heard on the news has been the fires."

"There's so much fire coverage, I'm not sure it was even on the news," Mary said. "A policeman came by our office with flyers this morning. He's canvassing the neighborhood, asking if anyone had seen her. They're treating it as a missing persons case, but the officer told me she was the fifth one in this part of the Valley. He was concerned. I could tell."

"Five! That's news to me." Kate stared idly out the window, watching an over-worked DWP crew pull into the nearby burger joint's drive-through. She thought back. "I only remember hearing about two women missing. Didn't know a connection might exist."

"So far the police don't have much evidence of anything, I think. Just the pattern might mean trouble. These weren't women who'd run off with a boy friend or anything like that. Not without telling friends, or giving notice at work. They're all—you know—dependable." Mary paused. "They even looked a little bit alike, at least to my eye."

"You saw pictures?"

"Yeah," Mary nodded. Momentarily her attention was diverted by the arrival of lunch. Pulling chopsticks from their wrapper, Mary deftly selected a moist chunk of kung pao chicken. "It was weird," she added. "Those pictures sort of reminded me of you."

By mid-afternoon the residual chill of the restaurant faded away. Kate spent her time tracking the many details of a manufacturing operation. She found herself glancing up often, only to see Charles Leimon looking away. It was unsettling. She had good instincts about people; there was something odd about this man. I need a stretch, she decided, and more aspirin. Grabbing her purse, she headed for the ladies room.

Staring into the mirror, Kate pondered the conversation at lunch. Mary was the secretary at a trucking company nearby. She had experience, common sense, a good head on her shoulders. And yet, Kate realized, Mary was spooked when she'd spoken of Kate's resemblance to the missing women. OK, so it isn't a comfortable idea, but in an area the size of Los Angeles many women look like me. Ordinary, dark-haired, average women. Safety in numbers. No one works in a neighborhood like this without keeping their eyes open. The cloying perfume of cheap air freshener in the overheated ladies room was suddenly oppressive. Out in the hall, even the water in the cooler was the worse for the heat. Kate excavated two aspirin from her purse, swallowing them with the lukewarm water. It tasted flat. It tasted the way she felt. She returned to her desk.

Kate opened a drawer and put her purse away before she noticed. It wasn't a big thing. She glanced around the large room. Most of the other people were busy at their jobs, trying to concentrate despite the heat. The Boss had the door to his office closed, the better to keep the cooling to himself. Charles was nowhere to be seen, but Ernie was gone, too, so they were probably out in the warehouse.

Kate looked back down at her desk. By the phone were two small candies. Lemon drops. They were ordinary things in an ordinary place. But they were out of place. A coldness touched her spine.

"Luvie," she called to the older woman on the other side of the low divider, "Did you put these candies on my desk?"

The bookkeeper turned from her work. "Candies? No way am I having anything to do with candies. I still gotta loose ten pounds before my daughter's wedding." She laughed. "I don't let myself get anywhere near temptation these days, Kate."

"Did you see anybody putting something on my desk?"

"Not this time of the month. I gotta get all the forms filled out for the tax people, plus keep up with the payroll processing. But everybody is always back and forth here anyway. Anybody could have put candies on your desk. Maybe you got yourself a secret admirer, eh?"

"If I have a secret admirer, he's so secret even I don't know about him yet," Kate said, feigning lightheartedness. She knew Luvie was right about people moving around the office. It might have been anyone. It's only a couple of candies, she told herself. Why am I so spooked about a couple of lousy candies?

She wrapped the candies in a tissue and dropped them into the waste basket. The uneasiness did not go away.

* * *

The rush hour news was filled with breathless reporters providing live coverage of the rampaging fires. "Crews and the equipment to fight them are in short supply. Gusting Santa Ana winds continue to relentlessly suck the moisture from everything. Summer dry hills of native chaparral are tinder. One spark is all these winds require, and sparks are frequent— from lightening, arcing power lines, carelessness, or arsonists." Kate felt the effects of the Santa Anas. Her skin dry, her hair like straw, there was static everywhere. Winds strong enough to blow down trees and swat eighteen wheelers off freeways play havoc with people's nerves as well. That's what it is, she told herself. These damned winds are getting to my nerves.

Near home, Kate stopped at the supermarket. She hit the aisles like a commuter hits the freeway, knowing exactly where she was going and the best route to get there. A glimpse of a face that might have been Charles Leimon's was quickly dismissed. He wasn't unique in appearance, and even creeps have to shop. In twenty minutes she was back at her car.

Though the sun was setting, heat radiated off the black-top. San Fernando Valley temperatures hovered in triple digits, despite the gusting winds. She loaded the bags into the trunk rapidly, eager to drive home in air-conditioned comfort. The car was an oven when she slipped into the driver's seat. Starting the engine to get cool air flowing, Kate realized she was sitting on something. She shifted her weight, running one hand under her. It felt like a couple of pebbles. Then Kate saw her mistake. Lemon drops.

* * *

"Exhausted fire crews continue to struggle against the fury of nature . . ." The radio reporter's voice died as Kate cut the engine in the company parking lot. The faint scent of smoke hung in the morning air making every breath a further aggravation to her scratchy throat. As she locked her car, wind-driven debris tumbled past her feet.

"It's a wonder there's anything left loose to blow around, isn't it?" a voice asked from a few yards away. It was Charles. "By now it must be rolling in from out of state."

Startled, she turned in his direction, her heart pounding. Kate hadn't noticed his car when she'd driven up. "Yes," she agreed lamely. "I . . . I have to get hold of someone on the East Coast. Ah . . . excuse me." She hurried into the building without looking back. The reflection in the window by the entrance showed her Charles was not following. As the door closed behind her, Kate slowed and forced herself to breathe deeply. The air conditioning had kept some of the smoke at bay. Her throat felt less abused inside the dingy walls.

The Boss was standing near the water cooler as she passed. "Join me?" he asked, holding up an empty paper cup. "Thanks," Kate replied. Normally his clumsy attempts at 'rubbing elbows with the troops' were something she'd tactfully avoid. Today even small talk at the water cooler with The Boss was a welcome respite. A guy with little talent for business, or the sense to realize that fact, he was a dud, but he wasn't a threat. She accepted the water, smiled politely, and made small talk.

Throughout the day Kate found herself stretching to ease tense muscles. When the telephone allowed, she walked around, just to see her little world from a different angle. She drank a lot of water.

"What is the matter with you today, Kate?" Luvie asked. "You been a nervous mess all day."

"Nervous?" Kate had hoped not to be so obvious. She lied, "It's these damned Santa Anas. I'm not really nervous. They just make me feel twitchy. You know . . ." She said nothing about lemon drops mysteriously appearing in odd places, and only to her.

"I see," Luvie said, clearly unconvinced. "It's the winds." The ringing of Kate's phone gave her an out. She answered it with relief and was soon embroiled in the problems of a wild-cat strike at a critical supplier. It was real and serious and everyday, the sort of problem that makes or breaks small business. It was a blessing. Kate let go everything else plaguing her mind to deal with the crisis.

By the time she hung up the phone, Kate realized hours had passed. Outside, darkness had fallen. Somewhere back in the manufacturing area a small second shift was working, but in the administrative area she was alone. Her mind still focused on the near-disaster she'd managed to avert, she gathered her things and left the building. Walking briskly to her car, the ever-present wind whipped grit into her face.

"I've been waiting for you," she heard Charles' voice from behind her. Kate turned toward him, alarm showing on her face. He'd moved his car during the day, she observed. She hadn't noticed it parked off in a corner of the lot.

Her back was to her locked car, the keys still in her purse. He was uncomfortably close. He reached out his right hand toward her, palm up. Lemon drops. "We have to talk," he said.

The tension of the past days flowed into Kate's mind, converting instantly to anger. "YOU!" she responded in a loud voice. "How dare you play these games with me! Who in hell do you think you are!"

Charles took a step closer. "I've been watching you. You're a special woman," he was saying in a calm voice, his hand still extended.

"I'll give you special!" Kate said angrily. Pulling her large purse off her shoulder with one hand, she swung it at his head. Thrown off balance by her unexpected reaction, Charles tried to duck. Using the momentum of her body, Kate grabbed his arm and pivoted. The attack sent him crashing head-first into the fender of her car. Like a large scarecrow, he slid to the ground near her front bumper. He moaned once, then lay still.

Keeping herself well back, Kate dug desperately into her purse for the car keys. She wasn't taking the chance of any further threats to her safety.

The silver Mercedes pulling into the lot was a welcome sight. "I was just coming back to pick something up," The Boss said. "I saw what happened. Get in, let me get you to someplace safe, and we can call the police from there. The cops can pick this guy up at any time." He leaned across to open the passenger door for her.

Kate jumped at the chance. A familiar face. Even if the face was The Boss. "Thanks," she said, slipping into the car. For once she meant it.

"I'll take you to my place," he said. "In the hills north of here. The guy doesn't know where I live, and there's a gate. When you feel better we'll call the cops to get this garbage.

"You know, I saw this guy watching you. I just didn't realize . . . I'm so sorry."

As The Boss talked, Kate was content to let him take control. She felt drained and weak. Her conscious mind seemed at a distance from her body, merely an observer watching the world move past the car windows.

They climbed into the hills on a twisty road and turned into a private driveway. The gates closed automatically behind them as they drove through a small orchard. The trees screened the property beyond from prying eyes. Sitting by itself on a ridge pointing south, the large Mediterranean style house overlooked the San Fernando Valley. The view was magnificent. "We'll go to the study," The Boss said. He parked the car in the turnaround, escorted her out of the car and into the house. "I'll get you a drink or a cup of coffee—whatever you want. You just relax. There's nothing to worry about here."

As he spoke he guided her by the arm through the house. Kate noted the tasteful decor. Part of her mind decided this must be his father's house. The Boss's sensibilities were not this refined.

The study was a corner room on the second level. Done in dark woods and rich leathers, it was very much a gentleman's environment. Kate sank gratefully into a chair by the fireplace. Near the windows, carved chairs and a matching table were ready to accommodate players of the chess game set up and waiting. While one large window revealed only the shadows of the wind-tossed orchard, the other was all glittering lights. This was a haven.

The Boss dropped his keys onto the desk. "Look, call me Jerry. This isn't work. This is a very different situation and I want you to be comfortable. What can I get you?" He opened hidden doors to reveal an expansive bar. "I got scotch. I got brandy. There's even some vintage port, if you'd prefer. Coffee, maybe. Food?"

"I'd love some coffee, if you don't mind," Kate said. "Caffeine before I faint."

"Fine," The Boss said. "I'll just go down to the kitchen and be right back. Don't you worry." He walked to the door, closing it behind him.

Kate didn't have the energy to worry. She was limp with relief. The creep would be dealt with. Soon the Santa Anas would die down, as they always did. People would go on with their lives. Even the prospect of calling The Boss 'Jerry' she could live with.

Feeling less stressed and more human, Kate looked around some more. A richly carved box sat on a low table. She tried to guess its place of origin. The workmanship was masterful. She reached over to examine it more closely. The lid came off.

Time stopped. Lemon drops! The box was full of lemon drops.

The lid slipped to the floor as Kate stood up. Her mind rejected what she was seeing. Without conscious thought she moved to the door and turned the knob. Locked!

Her muscles froze. What is happening to me? she wondered. Then, from the other side of the door, she picked up the sound of approaching footsteps. Instinctively she moved across the room near the game table.

"Here's your coffee. I hope you like it strong," The Boss said as he entered, carrying a tray. He set it on the desk, then looked at her. "What's wrong?"

Kate was speechless. She could only stare at him.

The Boss noticed the lid on the floor, and the now-open box. Something changed in his demeanor. Something unpleasant, almost reptilian. He turned to face her. "So," he said, "you know."

Kate nodded.

"I don't want to hurt you, Kate . . . I've always liked you. You just didn't seem to notice."

Kate said nothing.

"You're so competent. You handle things, Kate. That's never been easy for me. We'd make a good team, you know. I'm a nice guy. You'll see. You'll see how much I've learned from the others, and you'll learn to like me." He began to move toward her, slowly, like a snake approaching its prey.

That was it. Kate felt something inside her break free. She found her voice, and it was strong. "What the hell do you think this is?" she demanded.

He stopped. "I love you." He moved toward her again, a wild look in his eyes.

Kate thought of the missing women. "You son-of-a-bitch!" she yelled. She grabbed a chessman and threw it. Then she grabbed something else. Everything loose and liftable became a weapon, and she made full use of them, bouncing all sorts of objects off her would-be attacker.

The assault made him duck and wince. It stopped his advance. He was bleeding. And she was empty-handed. The floor was littered with objects, all out of reach.

"I love you!" he repeated.

Kate grabbed one arm of a chair. Its weight was awkward. Fear drove her beyond thought. She swung the chair like a hammer-thrower, using its weight as a counterbalance.

Sensing her fear, The Boss moved closer. The chair leg caught his knee. The popping sound was almost lost in his scream of pain. He went down.

As he collapsed, Kate gave one final heave, releasing the chair toward the window. With a splintering sound, the glass shattered, the chair flew outside. Heat-laden Santa Anas roared into the house.

Avoiding the fallen man, Kate snatched up her purse and his keys, then ran to the window. The tile roof four feet below the sill looked slippery, but safer than passing her writhing adversary to get to the door. Climbing over the sill, she heard him cry out behind her, "But I love you!"

The tile roof was tricky footing, but survival is strong motivation. At the edge she looked down. A one story drop. It was a gamble. Beats staying here! she told herself. She grasped the car keys in her teeth, rolled onto her stomach and let herself slide feet first over the edge, into a flower bed below.

Any landing you walk away from . . . popped into Kate's mind as she picked herself up. Her hands shook as she started the Mercedes. Twisting the wheel sharply, she accelerated away from the house and up the driveway toward freedom. Ahead, the locked gates barred her way. "But not for long," Kate said, flooring the accelerator and aiming for what she hoped was the weakest point.

The car took out the gate in a shower of sparks. The air bag deployed, startling her. Kate struggled to bring the car to a stop at the side of the road. "Let's hear it for German engineering . . ." she said, with a sense of exhilaration. Pushing the now deflated air bag out of her way, she got out of the car to look back.

The wind had picked up the sparks; the orchard was already starting to burn, tongues of flame reaching toward the house. This was no time to hang around. She heaved the twisted remains of one gate off the hood of the car and jumped back into the driver's seat. Ignoring the increasing glow behind her, she sped down the twisting road as fast as she dared.

Rounding one last turn, she was nearly blinded by the flashing lights on several cars speeding toward her. Slamming on the brakes, Kate ran—almost literally—into the police. With Charles Leimon.

He was wearing a badge.

* * *

". . .And in a bizarre story coming out of the San Fernando Valley, homicide investigators have located the remains of a man killed when wild fire swept his hill-top estate. Experts on the scene are checking out a gruesome discovery; what appear to be five shallow graves hidden in the burned over orchard on the property. More at eleven . . ."

Susam M. Stephenson:

Susan Stephenson has written PR professionally (including a fan club, pamphlets translating "medicalese" into English, advertising for orchid shows) and in her extensive volunteer work. Her articles on orchid growing have been published by the American Orchid Society. Her current project: a mystery novel set in the exciting world of orchids.

For information about the Sisters in Crime national organization, please contact:

M. Beth Wasson, Executive Secretary
PO Box 442124
Lawrence, KS 66044-8933
(785) 842-1034
sistersincrime@juno.com
<www.sistersincrime.org>

Books in Print

<http://www.books.com/sinc/authors.htm>

<http://www.books.com/sinc.yajuv.htm>

The Central Coast Chapter of Sisters in Crime is dedicated to promoting published and pre-published writers. With your support, we can offer new programs to meet this goal and continue to participate in projects such as our anthologies, Authors' Days, and the San Luis Obispo Book & Author Festival.

For more information about the Central Coast Chapter of Sisters in Crime, please contact:

Sisters in Crime
Central Coast Chapter
PO Box 1280
Grover Beach, CA 93483

ABOUT SISTERS IN CRIME

by Victoria Heckman

Sisters in Crime began in 1986 at the Baltimore BoucherCon when a number of women who read, write, buy or sell mysteries met for an impromptu breakfast to discuss their mutual concerns. At a minimum, they hoped to develop camaraderie and to learn what women in the mystery field really wanted. There was a perception that women writers were reviewed less frequently and their books were taken less seriously than those written by men.

Sara Paretsky was the driving force in galvanizing and organizing the group. In May of 1987, the first steering committee was elected.

In 1989, in the desire to be for its members, Sisters in Crime redoubled its efforts toward networking, publicizing its members' work, and lending mutual support.

The purpose of Sisters in Crime is to combat discrimination against women in the mystery field, educate publishers and the general public as to inequalities in the treatment of female authors and raise the level of awareness of their contribution to the field.

Membership in Sisters in Crime is open to all persons, worldwide, who have a special interest in mystery writing and in furthering the purposes of Sisters in Crime.